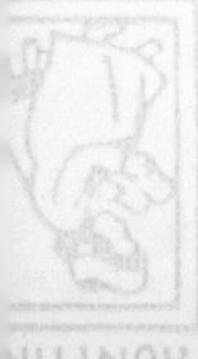

Mist *on the* Mountain

Mist *on the* Mountain

written and illustrated by JANE FLORY

HOUGHTON MIFFLIN COMPANY BOSTON

Books by

Jane Flory

Peddler's Summer

A Tune for the Towpath

One Hundred and Eight Bells

Clancy's Glorious Fourth

LIBRARY OF CONGRESS CATALOG CARD NUMBER 66-12097
PRINTED IN THE U.S.A.
SECOND PRINTING R

For my mother,

Hettie's youngest daughter

1

AMANDA leaned out the attic window and shivered a little. The September dawn was still chilly. The early morning mists clung damply to the top of the mountain, but as she watched the fog lightened and thinned and began to drift. Ragged wisps tore off and floated by, and through the torn places she could see first the dim outline of the huge maple that towered over everything at the edge of the clearing, and then the shapes of the outbuildings — the barn, the chicken coop, and Delcy's pigsty. The open yard between the house and barn was still shrouded and blurred, but the shaggy asters were there, Amanda knew, and the last of the black-eyed Susans. Ma loved flowers and always had a garden, but this last summer had been such a busy one that there was no time at all for luxuries like flowers. So the borders had gotten out of hand. The bee balm had seeded itself all over the clearing and fought the tangle of grass for a place in the sun. The lemon lilies had escaped from their neat clump at the door and were rioting shamelessly wherever they could find a toehold. Amanda didn't care. She liked things to be wild and free, and even flowers, she thought, must get tired of being confined to straight beds.

The Scoville farmhouse was not on the very top of the mountain. It snuggled into a hollow about a quarter of the way down, and behind the house rose the tree-covered hilltop, burning with autumn color as the morning sun touched the leaves. The house had its back against the mountain for protection from the winter winds. Its face looked out across the small fields that Pa had wrestled away from the woods, down the sloping hillside pasture and out to the valley below.

Amanda could see it all now — the green pasture grass, where Bossy and her calf Belva would soon graze, and the quiet little valley beyond. The farms looked like toys, with toy houses and toy people and animals. The Nixon boys were up and had milked already. She could hear the distant clanging of the cowbells and faraway shouts as they turned their herd out to pasture. Farther down was Julia's house, shining gold now as the sun reached into the valley. And the Moore place and the empty schoolhouse and all the rest.

Amanda leaned her elbows on the window sill and breathed deeply of the scented morning air. In a few more minutes everyone would be up and the house would hum with activity. Ma and the rest of the family would all have chores to do and there would be no time for dreaming. So she enjoyed it while she could, knowing that it wouldn't last much longer.

In the bed behind her, Mary stirred in her sleep and rolled up more firmly in the covers. Hettie and Sarah slept on quietly in the other bed. Amanda started to dress, moving as softly as she could so as not to waken them. They needed their sleep, all of them, and besides she liked the feeling of being the only one up so early.

When Pa died a year ago, taken sick so suddenly of the fever and gone before they could believe it, Ma was left with eight little girls to raise all alone. Emily, the youngest, was only a toddler and the twins, Teen and Toon, were hardly more than that. Then came Mary, now seven, and frail little Nan who was almost nine, and Amanda, going on ten. Hettie and Sarah were thirteen and past fifteen, tall strong girls, and capable.

Somehow they had managed to divide the chores and work together in spite of their grief and shock, and though it had been a struggle, they survived.

"It was because Ma never lost her spirit," Amanda decided, thinking about the hardships of last winter. "She never took time to feel sorry for herself and never let us feel that way either. That's the only way we did it."

Though the pain of missing Pa never really stopped, Amanda could look forward to the next winter with pleasure. It had been a good summer. Just enough rain and plenty of sun. Wonderful growing weather. The fields had done well and the woods, too. There was an abundance of the grains and vegetables and fruits they had grown with their own hard labor, and great quantities of nuts were in the woods above the house, just waiting to be picked and stored.

Best of all they had a little money, too. Amanda had worked all summer with a traveling peddler and had come home with thirty-two whole dollars! It was more cash then they had seen for a long time and it would get the few store-boughten things they needed to carry them through the winter. One of these days they would hitch Royal George to the wagon and drive down to the store in Waterton for shoes and new school books for Hettie and Sarah.

Mr. Aaron the old peddler, had insisted on leaving them with a parting gift of salt and nails and spices and would take no payment, even though Ma tried to insist.

"You vimmen," he laughed. "You are all alike. A penny burns a hole in your pocket. You should hoard your money and pay only for what you must. Take my gift as I give it, from the heart, and save the dollars for horse shoes and girl shoes which I haf not." So Ma had laughed, too, and had given in. She was proud and hated to be thought an object of charity, but loving kindness was something else again.

And so they were ready, and when the winter winds came and the snow and the biting cold, they wouldn't have to shiver and worry with one eye on the flour barrel and the other on the dwindling woodpile.

The sunlight came through the window and fell on Mary's face. She stirred and started to waken. At the same time Amanda heard a rope bed groan and the floor boards creek downstairs and then Ma's voice singing softly,

"Arise and shine and turn your face to God,
Arise and shine and thank Him for this day —"

It was Ma's favorite hymn and she sang it every morning, first softly to herself and then at the top of her voice to waken all the sleepers. It didn't matter whether the day was fine or miserable, whether it was to be a day of rest and pleasure or of hard backbreaking work, Ma sang her thanks.

Her spirit was catching. It was hard to be grumpy and cross in the face of such enthusiasm. Once in a while Amanda suspected that Ma's heart really wasn't in it, that she sang to hide her grief and her uncertainty. Maybe she would have liked to slam the frying pan and kick a stubborn piece of kindling wood, as Amanda often did. But Ma sang anyway to set a good example.

Not that Ma was always sweetness and light. Not by a long shot. She could come down like a stone boat on anyone who needed it. She couldn't abide laziness or sassiness or meanness, and she let people know it.

"Arise and *shine!"* she sang now, and there was no doubt that she meant it.

"Close your mouth, Mary, and wake up," said Amanda, already half out of her nightgown and into her shirt and underdrawers. "Everyone's been up for hours and you're still lying around like Delcy."

Mary shot upright in bed.

"Why didn't you call me, you mean hateful old thing," she sputtered. Her indignation fizzled out as she looked over and saw Hettie and Sarah sleepily rubbing their eyes. "Oh, you!"

Amanda grinned. It was fun to tease Mary and easy, too. Ma squelched it whenever she could, but there were plenty of times when Ma wasn't around.

"Stop it, Amanda." Sarah was next in command. It

was understood that the younger ones were to obey her when Ma was elsewhere. They grumbled sometimes at being bossed by one so young, but they obeyed. Sarah spoke gently but firmly, and really, she was right. So Amanda said no more to Mary at the moment and helped her with the back buttons on her petticoat.

It didn't take long for any of them to dress. It was only September and still warm enough to go barefoot. Hair took longer than clothes, for they all had long fine hair that tangled easily. Amanda shared the new hairbrush Mr. Aaron had given her with the "upstairs girls," as Nan called them. Ma, Nan, Teen, Toon, and Emily used the old one downstairs.

Hettie whipped the brush carelessly through her black hair and was off down the narrow winding stairs to the kitchen and out to the barn. Sarah smoothed her dark red hair until it shone like the polished mahogany table in Mrs. Nickerson's dining room. Then she dashed for the barn. She and Hettie milked Bossy and turned her and her calf Belva out to pasture each morning. Later they would give Royal George his measure of oats, but for now the old horse was happy in the pasture and needed no attention.

Amanda pulled Mary's yellow hair back with a ribbon and curled the ends around her finger. "There, you're ready. So are the chickens and I'll feed the pigs in a minute."

It took only a minute to braid her hair into two long pigtails, and she was off after Mary. She raced through the big downstairs room that was kitchen and dining room and living room for the Scovilles. She waved at Nan and Ma as she passed. She would say good morning properly when her chores were done.

Ma had something on her mind. All through breakfast she had a secret twinkly look, but only after the dishes were washed and the beds made did she make her announcement.

"Slick up, girls," she said. "Sarah, please hitch Royal George to the wagon. We're off to Waterton for horse shoes and girl shoes, as Mr. Aaron put it."

Then there really was excitement. Hair to be brushed again, best dresses on — the best they had, for no one but Emily had more than two. Emily fell heir to the twins' dresses so she always had an extra. They had already decided whose last year's shoes would fit whom, after much squeezing of reluctant toes.

Ma would wear her Sunday best kid boots and the cobbler in Waterton could resole her heavier winter ones. For barn and field chores she stuffed rags into the tips of the high boots that had been Pa's. They were awkward and uncomfortable but it was a great saving of shoe leather. Sarah had grown much taller over the summer and her shoes were not nearly big enough. Hettie had shot up, too, and Sarah's cast-off shoes didn't fit her either. Ma sighed and added another name to the list. Amanda could wear Hettie's, though, if the right heel was fixed, but Mary's feet were shorter and broader and nothing they could do would make Amanda's shoes comfortable for her.

Nan's narrow little foot slipped right into the pair

Amanda had worn two years ago. All outgrown shoes were carefully cleaned and oiled to keep the leather from cracking. Sooner or later someone would grow into them if they were stored properly away from too much heat or moisture. In the Scoville household, nothing was ever thrown away or wasted. A hand-me-down dress was taken as a matter of course. Old wool shawls were unravelled and knitted into new ones. So a brand new garment of any kind was a real event to look forward to. Mary could rejoice when Sarah got a new warm wool school dress for she knew that eventually it would be sponged and brushed and taken apart and made over to fit her.

The mountain lane was so steep that they all walked down to spare Royal George's strength. He was not a young horse, and the rocky little road would have been hard for the friskiest colt. Ma carried Emily although the little girl was able to walk. She was still apt to stumble, and she stopped every other step to pick up a shiny pebble or a pretty flower. It was slow going, so Ma carried her and they hurried down the road behind the empty wagon.

At Three Corners their lane met the valley road and the going was easier. They all climbed in the wagon and rode in bumpy comfort, waving now and then to their neighbors as they passed. Ma waved, but clucked George on, for Waterton was still a good seven miles away, and George as well as the girls had to be shod before nightfall. If they stopped to visit at every gate, the day would be over before it had begun.

As they jogged along, Amanda straightened her sun-bonnet to keep the bright sun out of her eyes, and swayed sleepily to the uneven rhythm of the wagon. She thought back to the enchanted summer just over, fondly but without regret. She missed Mr. Aaron, of course. He had come to be such a large part of her life that it seemed strange not to have him around. But there were other pleasures ahead — school and school friends, the first snow of winter — and there would be more summers selling sewing machines from the high red peddler's cart.

Old Mr. Aaron had stopped off with them for a few days when he brought Amanda home. He was at the end of his annual round and on his way back to his winter visit with his niece in Philadelphia. He had plenty of time for the trip back before cold weather and he could make the return journey slowly. His big peddler's wagon was almost empty. It was light and easy for Dobbin to pull. All the clocks and the sewing machines were sold, most of the clanging pots and pans and tools, all but a few brooms and bolts of cloth and some odds and ends.

Mr. Aaron had planned to give each girl a length of wool for a school dress but Ma was firm.

"You have done much more for us than you should, dear Mr. Aaron. None of us will go cold this winter, and it is better if we earn our own dresses with our own labor."

Mr. Aaron had given in for the moment. But wise old fox that he was, he had bested Ma in the end, and in a clever way, too. He had wrapped up a beautiful piece of black wool, along with yards of black braid and little ball fringe to trim it. He put in a paper pattern, much traced around by many customers. It was for a pelisse for Ma. Amanda knew what a pelisse was. Time after time during her summer of peddling she had explained it to farm women hungry for news of the latest fashion.

"A dear little short cape, ma'am, with rounded shoulders and a stylish small collar. You can make it with buttons down the front or with braid frogs to fasten it, and it's simply handsome trimmed with this fine ball fringe," she told them.

Mr. Aaron reasoned that if Ma found the gift after he had left she'd have to accept it. And she'd have to make it up for herself, since black was too somber for little girls and most appropriate for a widow. So he wrapped the package securely and placed it in the hollow of the big maple tree. As he left he handed Ma a note. On the envelope he had written in his beautiful flowing foreign hand, "Not to be Opened Until Exactly One Hour from the Time of My Departure. With Most Sincere Respects from an Ancient Admirer."

How he must have chuckled in his long gray beard, knowing how puzzled Ma would be as they waited out the hour and opened the mysterious letter.

Reach into the hollow tree
And find a Gift from Me to Thee.
I will be too far away
For you then to say me Nay.
I hope you do not think me wicked
Because so neatly you I trick-ed.
Please wear it with Joy and Health,
Like a Grande Dame of Greatest Wealth.

Ma couldn't be anything but pleased as she followed the instructions inside and found the little bundle in the tree. As Mr. Aaron had written, he was by then too far away for any protest. She laughed heartily over his funny verse and then smiled as she smoothed the rich black wool. It was a luxurious piece. Amanda knew it was cut from one of Mr. Aaron's most costly bolts of cloth. It would make up into a beautiful cape and Ma would look elegant in it.

"It's pure vanity, I know, and I should be ashamed of myself to be clothes-proud," Ma said as she held the material up against her. "But I can't help thinking how nice it will be for visiting and church doings. It'll wear for years," she added practically as if to make up for her lapse into frivolity. "Sarah and Hettie can borrow it when they get older."

Amanda was so busy thinking about the past summer that she was startled when Royal George whinnied and came to a stop.

"Here we are," said Ma. And there they were, right in front of the blacksmith's shop with the sign "Benj. L. McClellan, Smith" over the open door.

Mr. McClellan was sweating the rim on a wagon wheel. Sparks poured from his anvil as his son pumped furiously at the bellows to blow up the fire and he hammered away at the iron rim. When he saw Ma he waved his hand and put down his work. Ma averted her eyes modestly from his broad bare chest, covered only by the bib of his leather apron, and asked,

"Have you time to shoe our horse, Mr. McClellan?"

"Indeed I have, Miz Scoville." His answer came in a deep voice, rumbling out of that big strong chest. "And if I didn't have time, I'd make it. In town for a bit of shopping? You're all looking fine, just fine. Leave your wagon here and I'll have young Benjy drive it over to the General Store if you're not back by the time I'm finished. How are you, horse? Not showing your age none, I notice. Not like the rest of us." His laugh rang out as he patted Royal George. Mr. McClellan was really fond of animals. He cauld handle the wildest horse or mule, and he kept up a steady flow of reassuring talk to the animal as he worked. Young Benjy began to unhitch and Ma and the girls clambered down from the wagon. Amanda wanted to stay and watch and she protested when Ma motioned for her to come along.

"Pa always let me . . ."

"Your Pa stayed to watch, too," Ma murmured. "A smithy is no place for a young lady to hang around with rough man-talk going on. Come along."

Since young Benjy hardly said anything but "Yes, Paw," and "No, Paw," and Mr. McClellan carried on his conversation entirely with Royal George, Amanda couldn't see that there would be much man-talk. She liked the excitement of the hammer clanging on the anvil and the flying sparks, and the wild hissing as the smith thrust the red hot horse shoe into the waiting tub of cold water. But Ma said no, so she sighed and followed the others.

Waterton was not much of a town. A few houses set close to the road, the cobbler's shop, a general store that was also the post office, the blacksmith shop, a sign in a parlor window that said "Miss Adriana Allen, Milliner" —and that was it. Amanda had passed through many larger towns during her summer of peddling. But only passed through. There was no need for Mr. Aaron to stop in a community that already had the convenience of a general store. He avoided towns where he could and stuck to the more isolated areas where farmers and their wives waited eagerly for his arrival to stock up on all their needs. So for Amanda, as well as for the rest of the Scoville family, shopping in Waterton was an event and an adventure. She forgot her disappointment about the smithy and felt excitement rising inside her as they followed Ma into the cobbler's shop.

The cobbler agreed that he could fix their shoes right away since they had made such a long trip to town. He would let some of his closer customers wait a little, he said kindly. It would have been fun to linger here, too, and watch the little old man work, but the pull of the store was even stronger. That was where she wanted to go.

The store bell jangled as they went in the door. Teen and Toon were inclined to go in and out, just to make the bell ring, but Hettie had one by each hand and she put a stop to that.

Ma's shopping list was short. They supplied most of their wants at home and Mr. Aaron had taken care of some of the extras. But it was fun to go to the store anyway, even if they didn't need a lot. They waited while the storekeeper took care of a fussy customer and then Ma stepped up to the counter with her list.

Amanda looked around the cluttered store with a practiced eye. After all, although her main reason for going with Mr. Aaron had been to demonstrate his wonderful sewing machines, she had learned to help him with all his selling. He had taught her the difference between a shoddy piece of material and the good quality that he preferred to carry, between a thinly tinned cooking pan and one that was well made and would last a long time. He had a better eye, too, for womanly notions, Amanda decided. Mr. Aaron stocked many small inexpensive items that were attractive and fanciful. Cooky cutters in every imaginable shape; beautiful rolls of ribbons and laces; elaborate buttons; little gold lockets. This merchant, she decided, was all right for the everyday things. He had a good stock of tools and lanterns, but she sniffed when she saw his line of dress-goods. He — or his wife, most likely — had the *frumpiest* taste. Nothing but plain serviceable homely browns and grays, not even the lovely colors that Ma could get from dyeing homespun with onion skins and beet root and sassafras bark. Mr. Aaron could sell rings around him, as well, for the storekeeper had a disgruntled manner that did not invite further sales. Funny what a nice, pleasant way about you could do to encourage people to buy. Mr. Aaron did it without even trying, just by being his own kind friendly self.

But this man did have shoes for sale, which Mr. Aaron did not. The space in the red peddler's wagon was so limited that he had decided shoes were unprofitable to carry. He would have to have so many sizes and shapes on hand that shoes alone would fill his wagon to overflowing. Besides, many farmers were also fair cobblers and made all the family shoes themselves.

Ma was asking now for shoes for Hettie and Sarah and Mary. The storekeeper measured their feet with a ruler and climbed his step ladder to get them down from their hooks on the rafters. They were nothing fancy, of course, just good strong black leather high-buttoned boots that would wear well. Not for them the soft French kid boots with scalloped trim worn by the ladies in Mr. Aaron's fashion books. Soft French kid would be cut to ribbons after a few trips up and down the rocky mountain lane, and as for shedding water — !

After the shoes, Ma ordered two barrels of coal oil. With careful filling and economical use of the lamps, that much would last a long time. There remained the school books. Here again there would be a great deal of handing down, but Sarah had advanced into a much harder arithmetic and Hettie needed a new reader. It was exciting to have brand-new books. Even the youngest girls patted the shiny new covers and the fresh clean pages.

After that there really wasn't too much to buy but they enjoyed looking around. The storekeeper made suggestions but Ma shook her head. Tools? Nails? Spices? They had a-plenty, thank you. Salt? Well — Ma hesitated and then decided two pounds more wouldn't go amiss even if Mr. Aaron had left them with a good amount. It would keep, and this might be a long winter. Sugar? There was a bee tree up in the woods that would supply them with honey enough for all their needs, and one of Mrs.

Nixon's sons had promised to cut it down for them. That would be all they needed, Ma told the storekeeper. He added up the bill and Ma had her purse open to pay when suddenly she changed her mind.

"Two cakes of lilac soap, please," she said, to the amazement of her children. Ma, who was always so practical! "And a twist of white sugar for the tops of cookies."

Mary gasped. White sugar was a real luxury, to be hoarded for very special occasions.

"Make it a good-sized twist," Ma added. "We're a good-sized family." The storekeeper measured out a generous scoop of sparkling white sugar onto a piece of paper and twisted it into a cone. He tucked in the ends securely so not one precious grain would spill and placed it carefully on the top of Ma's market basket. She paid the bill and bowed politely to the storekeeper. He bowed in return and hurried to open the door for them. He really wasn't such a cross man after all, Amanda thought. It didn't pay to judge people too quickly.

As they went out into the September sunshine Mary whispered to Amanda,

"Manda, are we rich?" It took Amanda a minute to think of the right answer. "It's hard to say," she finally decided. "Next to Mrs. Nickerson, I guess we'd be considered dirt-poor, she lives so elegant and fine. And next to the Newlands we'd be not so well off, what with their great big farm on nice flat land and all those boys coming along to help work it. But then there were others I met on my travels who didn't have much money, and not much fun at all. That's one thing we do have, lots of fun."

"Then we're rich," said Ma, who had overheard. "Lots of fun and love and songs, and things to wear and to eat, and a sound roof over our heads and mother-wit enough to fix the roof if ever it starts to leak. And a little spare cash for emergencies."

"And two whole beautiful cakes of lilac soap," breathed Nan happily.

"That's pure vanity," Ma sighed. "Every year if crops were good, your Pa always bought me two cakes of lilac soap. He knew how tired I get of the smell of homemade soap. I'm afraid I have a strong streak of vanity, much as I try to fight it." She frowned as if she were scolding herself and then smiled again. "We'll all share it for special occasions like the first day of school. You'll go off smelling like flowers."

School would start in a week, Amanda thought with pleasure. The summer had been wonderful, a summer to remember always, but a new school year was ahead and that would be wonderful too, in a different way. She thought of the first day of school, with the one-room schoolhouse still smelling of the strong soap and lye that Master Pulsifer had used to scrub it. Everyone would be dressed up, if not in brand-new school clothes, then in freshly starched and ironed hand-me-downs. Feet would ache in new shoes after a summer of barefooted freedom. They would be assigned seats — she hoped she and Julia could sit together again this year. If she had to share a seat with Alice she'd die — just die! Everyone would get to school extra early. They needed time to catch up on all the summer activities, for there wasn't much opportunity for socializing during the busy growing and harvesting season.

She would be the center of attention, she knew. She was the only one in the whole school who had gone off on a peddling trip and who had had so many adventures. Even the biggest boys and girls would gather around to hear about it, and the little ones would be goggle-eyed at all she could tell.

Then Master Pulsifer would ring the bell and they would hurry inside for the first classes of the new year. She could hardly wait!

Hettie had run ahead to the cobbler's shop to get the shoes. She caught up to the rest of the family as they walked down the main street of Waterton. While Amanda was thinking, they had come back to the place they started, at the blacksmith shop. Mr. McClellan had just finished shoeing Royal George. It was too bad to have missed it, but maybe next time she would be allowed to watch. Young Benjy hitched George to the wagon and helped them in without a word, for he was a very quiet young man. Ma paid Mr. McClellan for the job, thanked him, clucked to the horse and they moved off. They picked up the barrels of coal oil at the store and then turned toward home.

It took only a few minutes to leave the town behind them. Nan sighed, "We probably won't see Waterton again until next Spring," she said. "It's always over so fast."

They all felt a little let down. Mary was the practical one, as usual. "The longer you stay in a town, the more money you spend. I think we left just in time."

Everyone had to laugh at such down-to-earth wisdom coming from one so young.

"Anyway, I'm hungry and it's way past noon," Mary added. Hettie and Sarah opened the lunch basket and divided the food. They ate as they jiggled along and afterwards they started to sing "Froggie Would A-Wooing go." There were so many verses that the song lasted almost all the way home.

2

Mary panted up the hill and announced breathlessly, "Ma, when we passed the Moores' house on the way home, Mr. Moore said he was taking apples to the cider mill tomorrow and if we're ready he'll take ours, too!"

Ma wiped her soapy hands on her apron and stepped to the porch. "Mmm — sky's clear, not a cloud. It should hold clear through Saturday. Fine, then, we'll send the cider apples and the apple butter apples, too, and save ourselves a trip, as long as he's offered."

"What does the sky have to do with cider?" Mary was curious.

"Quite a lot. The cider you use for apple butter should be as fresh as possible — made the same day if you can, or the next day at the very latest — and our kettle is too big to stir comfortably in the fireplace so we'll have to make it outdoors, and for that we need a clear day. You see?"

Mary nodded. "And today is Thursday, and tomorrow

the cider will be made and on Saturday we'll all be home to help so it works out fine. I'll remember that when I'm grownup and making apple butter myself."

"You do that, Mary. And remember, you can't beat the recipe my grandmother handed down to us. Everybody thinks it's specially good."

There was a lot to do that afternoon. The "drops," the apples that had fallen from the tree and had been left to ripen in the tall grass, were already picked up and put in baskets in the barn, separated according to variety. Some people made cider out of any old apples, but Pa had always been fussy about the mixture he used, and Ma tried to remember exactly how he did it.

"Let's see, you use Baldwins and Russets for a good part of it, half, I'd say, and then mix in equal amounts of the rest — the Smokehouse and the Northern Spies and some Rome Beauties. Then for the apple butter cider we use only the Yellow Sweets. And sort them carefully, girls. Any that aren't just right put aside for Delcy."

Delcy was their big brood sow, fat and ugly but somehow lovable. Her full name was Delcina Del Di Bosa after an actress that Ma had read about. She preferred sweet apples to any other. Ma said it was because they pampered her and kept her contented that she had such good big litters of baby pigs. The girls were all careful not to get attached to the babies, cute as they were, for it was understood that they were to be raised for meat and butchered in the early winter. But Delcy was different. They had had her for years, and so they could give her a name and lavish attention on the homely creature. They had a boar, too, named Excelsior, but he was a cross old thing and not at all pleasant.

They worked hard and fast, all of them. Even little Emily had a small basket and made trip after trip to the pig pen to feed the bruised apples to Delcy. Hetty and Sarah fed the stock and did the evening chores, and by the time it was beginning to be dusk, the apples were ready for the mill.

Sunset came earlier down in the valley, but up on the mountain the sun lingered on the top of the hills. The trees were flaming with color and the golden light held a little warmth still. They watched for a moment, breathing in the sweet apple-scented air, and then Ma said briskly,

"My gracious, it'll be dark soon and we haven't even thought about supper. Let's hurry. We've another busy day tomorrow and the little ones are drooping on their feet."

Emily, indeed, was swaying sleepily and Ma scooped her up and carried her into the house. Amanda and Mary took the pails to the spring for water. They ran with the wooden buckets banging together, just one leap ahead of the darkness that was coming swiftly now. It was hard to walk back over the uneven path from the spring in the woods with full water pails and barely enough light to see by. Once Mary stubbed her toes on a root that twisted out into the path, and half a bucket of water sloshed over the side, but they still had enough for cooking and dishes and bedtime washing. They would go again in the early morning, for though a nip of autumn frost might be in the air, it was not cold enough yet to make even a thin film of ice. Later in the winter they would keep a supply of water in the house close to the warmth of the fire so it would not freeze. But the fiercely cold days of winter were still far off. Plenty of time to bundle up and shiver later on.

Amanda loved this time of day — if it was day — the time when the world hung between brightness and dark and couldn't seem to make up its mind which way to go. When they were not so rushed she always offered to go alone for the water so she could poke along on the way back. Tonight she was glad of Mary's help. All the water could be brought in one trip.

While Amanda and Mary were gone, Nan set the table and poured out big glasses of foaming milk that Sarah and Hettie had brought in from the barn. Mother had peeled and sliced a pan of apples and was browning them gently in butter in the three-legged iron spider in the fireplace. Corn meal mush was crisping in another iron frying pan, and there was, as almost always, a pot of soup bubbling in the big soup kettle.

All sorts of things went into the soup kettle — fresh vegetables in the summer, dried ones in the winter, bones of whatever meat they had. Sometimes the soup tasted mostly of ham and beans, sometimes the main flavor was chicken, less often a big beef bone simmered in the broth. But it was always thick and good and nourishing, flavored with a pinch of this and a dash of that. In the little attic storage room next to the upstairs bedroom bunches of herbs hung from the rafters. Some were gathered wild from the woods and some were carefully tended in Ma's little kitchen garden. They all added their sweet and pungent flavor to Ma's good cooking.

Tonight the soup was almost too thick to stir and needed a dipper of spring water to make it thin enough to ladle out into the soup bowls. The teakettle was filled and hung from the crane so it would be hot for washing dishes. After each one had washed and dried her face and hands and Ma had sponged off sleepy, grubby little Emily, they all sat down.

They bowed their heads while Ma asked the blessing and then, as quickly as was polite, they began to eat. They were too busy to talk very much for all of them were hungry and more than a little tired. Even before she had spooned up the last of her apples, Emily put her head on the table and was fast asleep.

"Good heavens," Ma laughed softly. "She'll have apples in her hair. I'll put her to bed while you all clear away. You come too, Teen and Toon, and no fussing. I see your eyelids drooping."

Ordinarily the lively little four-year olds would have protested at being put to bed with Emily. But tonight they slid off the bench obediently and followed Ma without a word. They were too drowsy to argue.

By the time Ma came back from tucking the three youngest children into bed, Mary, Nan, Amanda, Hettie, and Sarah had cleared the table and were washing the dishes in a basin at the wooden sink. In no time at all the dishes were dried and put away in the big cupboard and the long table was spread with books and copybooks and slates.

Ma sat in her rocker and knitted, ready to help when she was needed with the correct spelling of a hard word. She wrinkled her forehead with a puzzled frown when Sarah asked her about a problem in arithmetic.

"You girls have gone way beyond me in your sums," she said. "I had precious little schooling — not as much as Nanny even."

"But, Ma, you can spell us all down," protested Amanda.

"That was your Pa's doing. He was a great reader, you know, just loved books. If he'd had a proper chance, he'd have been a real scholar, maybe a professor somewhere. But here he was, stuck on a little mountain farm to scrabble for a living, so he scrabbled. But in his free time, and even some time when he wasn't free, he was busy reading everything he could get his hands on. Even when he was plowing, he'd sneak in a page or two at the end of each row. That's how he and Mr. Aaron got to be such good friends. Mr. Aaron had been loaning him books since he was a boy — bringing them on the spring trip and stopping to pick them up in the fall. I couldn't have your Pa ashamed because his wife never got beyond the Third Reader, so I read, too, until I could keep up with him. But sums still come hard to me."

They were all quiet for awhile, eyes full of tears, remembering their tall laughing father. Then practical little Mary wiped her nose on her petticoat hem and changed the subject in her business-like way.

"Mr. Moore and the boys are coming for the apples right after breakfast. He said they'd load the wagon for us."

Ma thought for a moment and then said,

"Hettie, you and Sarah must go along to the cider mill. I don't want all those apples dumped into the press helter-skelter. Mr. Moore's a good kind neighbor but he doesn't know beans about making cider, especially for apple butter. I wouldn't give a continental for Erna Moore's apple butter and I think it's because of the apples they use for cider."

Sarah looked dismayed.

"Oh, Ma, couldn't Hettie go alone? Master Pulsifer is giving us a review examination in geography tomorrow and he'll be cross as a bear if I miss it."

Hettie was just as dismayed.

"Sarah, you traitor!" she cried. "I'll have to go alone with those pesky little Moore boys and be nice and polite because Mr. Moore is doing us a favor, and all the while I'll be itching to knock their heads together!"

Mother was firm. "Then Amanda must go with you. Someone's got to keep my lovely sweet apples from getting mixed in with the others, else all the work of sorting them will be wasted. And you know how glad you'll be to have apple butter sandwiches in your dinner pails come wintertime."

Amanda was delighted. "Goody! We'll have a day off from school. It'll be a holiday!"

"Anything to get away from routine," Ma sighed. "You have a holiday heart, Manda."

"Is that a bad thing to have?" Mary asked, half hoping that it was.

"A holiday heart? No, not really. It's just that Amanda jumps at any chance to have a change, no matter what. I'd hate to have her turn out flighty like Evaline Pettingill with not a brain in her head because she never would buckle down in school."

Amanda sucked on the end of her slate pencil, her eyes dreamy. "I think it's a good thing to have. My friend, Mr. Padraic O'Leary, has one, I'll bet. Within a few minutes after we met him, he had bread and cheese tasting like a party, and I'm sure it was because he had a holiday heart. I'll bet he could make a trip to the cider mill seem as exciting as a trip to the moon — singing and playing all the way, and telling stories. Anyway, you don't need to worry about me. I won't be flighty like Evaline. I'll be busy all day helping Hettie keep a firm hand on William and Henry Moore."

"You see that you keep a hand *off* the Moore boys, do you hear? No knocking heads together, Hettie, no matter how they try your patience. A lady never strikes or pushes or shoves, no matter what."

"Or raises her voice. I know. But ladies can *look,* can't they? Every time one of those . . . those monsters gets out of hand we'll look at them with fire in our eyes and they'll get the idea."

"Amanda can give you a look that would kill a snake," said Mary. "She can shrivel you right up just by looking. Remember the time she . . ."

Ma cut short the reminiscence that was distracting

them all from their studying with a reminder that it was getting late and they could either finish their schoolwork or get up an hour earlier the next morning to do it. There was silence then for a long time, broken only by the squeak of slate pencils and an occasional moan of despair from Sarah who was memorizing her geography.

The clock — bought long ago from Mr. Aaron and one of the few possessions in the house that had not been made by Pa or Ma or others in the family before them — ticked loudly in the quiet room. When it struck nine, Ma put her knitting into the basket at her side and said,

"Time for the reading, children, and then to bed. Tomorrow will be another busy day." She opened the big family Bible and read a Psalm. Amanda followed the lovely words in the little red leather book that Aunt Jem Garrison had given her. Before she closed the smooth well-worn covers she said a quick prayer for Aunt Jem.

She saved Mr. Aaron and her family for the prayer she said on her knees at her bedside. Then she clambered in beside Mary and reached for her share of the coverlet. Somewhere nearby, probably in the big maple, a little screech owl called softly, and from far away came the sad, gentle answer.

The air was like honey, warm and sweet and golden. It seemed almost to have substance to it, as if it could be poured from a spoon. Amanda and Hettie bounced sedately on the front seat of Mr. Moore's wagon, with only an occasional glance back at the giggling Moore boys. Warm as it was, Ma had insisted they wear sunbonnets and light shawls, but the shawls soon slipped off their shoulders and before long the sunbonnets were pushed back from their perspiring foreheads.

Mr. Moore was a kindly man but not much of a talker so they rode along in silence. Amanda didn't mind. It was such a treat to have a day off that she felt no need to talk. She just rode along and enjoyed it. Mr. Moore had been eager to get an early start, for the trip to the cider mill, while not far, could easily become an all-day expedition. It was important to be on time. Late comers might wait for several hours before their apples were put through the press. Mr. Moore wanted to be sure to get both batches of apples pressed and kegged and carried home before chore-time.

The wagon bumped and banged over the rutted road. Hettie grabbed the edge of the wagon seat to hold on, and Amanda, who was sitting in the middle, held tight to Hettie. Once in a while when the road was more than usually bad and the going was slow, William and Henry jumped off and ran along beside the wagon.

"Whyn't you two get off and lighten the load?" Henry called. "Big Gray can hardly pull such a heavy load as you two."

"Wagon springs are mighty near breaking," added William. "They aren't used to haulin' fat old girls."

"We aren't fat," began Amanda, but Hettie hushed her with a poke in the ribs. Both girls ignored the boys and put their noses high in the air to show that they were above responding in kind to the boys' taunts. This was a mistake for it only spurred the boys on to greater efforts.

"Yes, ma'am, Your Royal Highnesses," said William cuttingly. "I guess Your Highnesses the Queen and the Princess are too good to ride in the back of the wagon with the poor common people."

Henry chimed in, "Wouldn't want to get your ermine cloaks all messy with apples."

Still the girls would not answer. Mr. Moore was deep in thought and paid no attention at all.

"When we get to the mill wouldst roll out the Royal Carpet so the Empress and the Grand Duchess won't soil their shoes, William, my good man?"

"Certainly, goodly knight Henry. The Grand Duchess can stand on the carpet as she throws golden apples at the poor miller's head."

Amanda was trying to think of a scathing answer when Mr. Moore beat her to it. He took his pipe out of his mouth and said,

"That'll be enough out of you two. Back in the wagon and quiet. Not another word out of either of you until we get to the mill." Then he turned to Amanda and said, "Seen you throw them golden apples, Amanda Jane. Never knowed you had such a good aim. Split my sides laughing." He put his pipe back in his mouth and was silent again.

Amanda's cheeks flushed with embarrassment. Although she had been assured over and over that the Myth of the Three Golden Apples had been the high spot of the Closing Day Program, and that possibly it had even saved Master Pulsifer from trouble with the school board, still she always thought of it as a dreadful disappointment. She was grateful to Mr. Moore, though, for quieting his boys. They said nothing to the girls for the rest of the trip and that was a blessing. They continued to whisper and snicker, and Amanda was sure they were up to something. She hoped that she and Hettie could cope with whatever plan they were cooking up.

William and Henry weren't really bad boys. Henry was Amanda's age and William a year younger. They were not good students, but neither were they the slowest in the class, either. But they were terrible teasers and practical jokers, and the minute they were out from under Master Pulsifer's watchful eye they were into mischief. They spent more time doing extra sums for punishment than any other children in the whole school.

Amanda had long ago decided that the best way to handle them was to ignore them, but it wasn't always easy to do. Once they found something to tease about, they clung to it as a puppy clings to a bone, pulling it this way and that. For Amanda the "bone" was the story of the mashed Golden Apples, and it seemed as if the Moore boys would never let it go.

To the girls' relief they soon turned into the lane toward the cider mill. The old stone mill was built beside a brook that came rushing down the hill. The brook water was channeled into a sluiceway that tumbled it over the water wheel when the old miller gave the signal to his helper. During the grain-grinding season the wheel turned huge millstones, and the race — the deep fast moving channel on the other side of the mill —

supplied the power. But cider making was a lighter job that could even be done by hand when a farmer had only a few apples.

Mr. Moore was pleased to see that only one wagon was waiting there in the lane. The horse was grazing on the grass beside the road and his owner's apples had already started through.

"Good timing," grunted the taciturn Mr. Moore. "We won't have to wait long." He waved a greeting to the miller and made himself comfortable on a bench in the sunshine, filled his pipe and settled down to wait his turn.

Amanda and Hettie got down from the high wagon seat, glad to stretch and walk around a little. It had been a long and bumpy ride and it felt good to stretch their legs. William and Henry had leaped from the back of the wagon even before it stopped and were already hanging over the railing, watching the pressing. They had all seen it before, of course. The cider making was a yearly occurrence that came as regularly as the apples. But it was always interesting.

First the apples were dumped in a box built on the hill behind the mill, and pushed along a wooden trough into another box where they would be ground. The old miller kept his eye on the apples tumbling down the slope and when enough of them were in the grinding hopper he motioned to his helper at the sluice gate. His helper pulled a lever that opened the sluice and let a stream of brook water burst through. As the water hit one of the paddles on the wheel it began to turn, and that moved the gear on the grinding box. In no time at all the apples were no more, crushed and smashed into a thick mass called pomace.

The miller and his helper worked swiftly now, shoveling layers of pomace onto burlap covered frames that, piled high one on top of another, made a filter holding back the thick part of the crushed apples, but allowing the juice to seep through. When the frames were full, the pressing began. Slowly, steadily, the miller walked round and round, pushing on the long wooden handle that turned the wooden jackscrew. The screw put pressure on the pomace covered frames. Round and round went the handle, and soon big bubbles of juice were pressed through the burlap. The clear amber juice began to drip out of the bottom, at first a few drops at a time and then a thin trickle that started to fill the big shallow tub beneath.

It was the same old scene they had watched year after year and yet to Amanda it always came as a surprise that the baskets and bumpy bags of hard apples could turn into this clear heavenly smelling juice. Her mouth watered for a taste, but there would be time for that later. For now, it was enough that the golden sun was warm on her back, that it warmed the sweet tangy air, warmed the old stones of the mill and touched them with gold. She leaned on the rail and felt as if she were touched with gold as well, as golden as the old miller, for he was golden, too. His apron was splashed with brown gold juice and pomace, his wrinkled old skin was sun colored. The miller went round and round and round. . . . Her half-dream was interrupted by a shout from William.

"That's all!" he said. "Our apples go through next."

The miller's helper had opened the wooden spigot in the tub and was filling the farmer's kegs, one after another. The pomace, squeezed of all possible juice, was scraped from the burlap frames and discarded on a heap. Mr. Moore and the boys began to unload their baskets at the box on the slope. The process was about to begin all over again.

"This wagon load all go in together?" asked the miller. Mr. Moore shook his head. "Nope, keep 'em separate. Miz Scoville's particular about her cider. Says it makes a difference what kinds of apples go in it."

The miller nodded approvingly at Amanda and Hettie.

"Then you're Scovilles, eh? Should have remembered, but you young'uns all grow so from one year to the next. Your Pa was particular, too, and that's how it should be."

Mr. Moore shifted his pipe and said.

"Never seems to make no difference to me — cider's cider is what I say. But we've plenty of time to be fussy. It's not even noonday yet. Ladies first. Us men'll wait."

Amanda watched their carefully picked-over apples roll and bump their way down the sloping trough into the grinding box. The miller gave the signal, the stream of water burst from the sluice gate and splashed against the water wheel and it began all over again. When the Scoville cider was finished, their apple butter cider went through. Mr. Moore squinted at the sun and said,

"Let's load the barrels on the wagon and then have a bite to eat. Sun's right overhead."

The miller and his helper went up the hill to the house for their dinner. Amanda and Hettie and the Moores opened the pails that had been filled for their noonday meal. Mrs. Moore had insisted that she would send dinner for all of them, and it was good. Ma might not give a continental for Erna Moore's apple butter, but everyone knew that she had the lightest hand with pie crust of anyone in the valley. Though no lighter than Ma's, Amanda thought loyally, but in all fairness she had to admit that the cold meat pasties were delicious. They washed them down with the last of the cider from the big barrel, dipping it out with the miller's worn wooden dipper.

All this time the Moore boys had been too engrossed with the business of cider making to pester the girls. Now that they had seen several batches of cider go through, and were full and contented, they returned to their usual behavior.

Mr. Moore was snoozing on his back in the sun, his burnt-out pipe forgotten beside him. Seeing his father safely asleep, William began,

"Well, Your Highness," he said to Amanda, "has Your Majesty had enough to satisfy your Royal Taste? Methinks you still seem thirsty."

"I've had a-plenty, thank you," said Amanda warily. William wasn't being polite for nothing. She wondered what was coming next.

"Oh, come on now, just a sip more of your extra special cider." He passed her the dipper and Amanda took it. It was so good, and the turnovers had been spicy. She bent to drink from the dipper and Henry pushed her head from behind. Her whole face went into the cider, — nose, mouth, eyes, even her ears were wet! Sputtering with rage and with the cider that had gone up her nose, she wiped her face on her sleeve. The boys were rolling on the ground with laughter.

"Look at the queen!" they gasped. "Old cider-ears!"

This was too much. Amanda knew the nick-name would stick if the boys started it at school. She would never be allowed to forget it. With both hands she swung the heavy dipper. Clunk! it thumped on William's head, and clunk! she cracked it on Henry.

They lay stunned for an instant while Amanda and Hettie looked at each other in horror. What had Ma said? Ladies don't push or shove or crack heads — and she had not only cracked their heads but maybe had split them altogether!

It was a short instant. William and Henry recovered quickly and set up a howl that resounded even above the rushing of the noisy brook. Mr. Moore opened his eyes.

"I seen it all, boys, and you had it comin' to you. Back in the wagon and shet up your hollerin'." He closed his eyes again, confident that his orders would be obeyed, and dozed off once more.

Amanda and Hettie silently gathered up the dinner pails and rinsed them in the cold brook water. Then

Hettie dipped the tail of her petticoat into the brook to wipe off the cider that was already beginning to dry stickily on Amanda's face. The pleasure had gone out of the holiday. The warmth of the sun and the good smell of cider had lost all their charm.

"Well, I fixed this day, didn't I?" Amanda asked gloomily. Hettie nodded and finished her scrubbing job without words. Amanda was right. She had spoiled the day.

The miller and his helper came back from their dinner and the process started again, this time with Mr. Moore's apples. Several more farmers had arrived and were waiting for their turns. It would be late when they finished, but perhaps they had someone at home to do the chores.

The Moore boys stayed in the wagon as they had been told, glowering furiously at Amanda and Hettie, but not saying a word. Their father ignored them completely until his cider started to trickle through the press into the low catching tub. Then he relented and called,

"Come on, get your straws if that's what you've been counting on. I reckon you've been punished long enough. But no nonsense, mind you, or *I'll* use the dipper on you next time."

With a whoop, the boys leaped off the wagon. They had collected a supply of oat straws for the cider sipping that traditionally ended each pressing. They dashed for the barrel and then remembered their manners — under their father's stern eye — long enough to offer straws to Hettie and Amanda. All hard feelings seemed to have been forgotten so the girls accepted and knelt on the mushy ground by the cider barrel. The cider was sweeter than ever, pulled through the oat straw. The effort of sucking it up made it even more worthwhile. Mr. Moore looked at the miller and grinned. The miller returned his smile.

"Three generations I've watched them doing that," he said. "These young'uns and their parents and their grandparents, too. And it's always the same, just like it was yesterday. Nothing like cider through an oat straw."

The children were not the only ones clustered around the cider barrel. The little yellow wasps had gathered in humming swarms attracted by the sweet smell and the piles of pomace nearby. They could be discouraged by a wave of the hand but it was important not to anger them by swatting. They were quick to sting when they were angry.

When William finally had his fill he wiped his mouth with the back of his hand. Unfortunately, at that very instant a wasp had lighted on the back of his hand, and for the second time that day William set up an ear-splitting howl. His lip was stung three times before he brushed the wasp away. Tears of pain and anger filled his eyes. Amanda scooped up a handful of the cider-softened earth by the barrel. With the other hand she dipped cold water out of the swiftly running sluice. In an instant she had a thick paste of mud and applied it liberally to his swelling lip.

"Mud is the best thing for stings," she explained. "It'll feel better in a minute."

The cider sipping was over. Mr. Moore and the miller

filled the cider kegs and loaded them on the wagon. Amanda made fresh poultices of mud to put on William's lip while Henry hovered sympathetically. Hettie suggested that one of the dinner pails could hold a supply of cool mud, enough to last all the way home, and Amanda could ride in the back of the wagon to change the mud-pack each time it started to dry.

Mr. Moore clucked to his horse and slapped the reins and they started on their bumpy homeward trip. Mr. Moore took his pipe from his mouth and said to Hettie, his eyes crinkling with amusement.

"Meek as Moses, ain't they? Looks like the cider war is over."

3

IT WAS HARDLY DAYBREAK when Ma called from the foot of the stairs, "Girls, get up! There's lots to do today and we want to get an early start." They tumbled sleepily from their beds into the chilly dawn and by the time the sun was starting to climb, their day was in full swing.

Sarah and Hettie raced to the barn to take care of the milking, Amanda fed Delcy and Excelsior, Mary scattered feed for the chickens and gathered the eggs in her apron. Nan dressed Emily and helped Teen and Toon with their back buttons and brushed hair all around. They were all finished and were washing up as Ma was putting their breakfast on the table.

"Eat hearty," she urged. "We'll have our noonday meal on the run, most likely, and stirring all day takes a heap of energy."

They didn't need her urging. Even Nan's finicky appetite was growing and she, too, passed her bowl back for a second helping of oatmeal.

They had sat up quite late the night before, peeling

apples. Ma had clamped the apple peeler onto the edge of the long table and divided the work so that no one did any job so long she got tired of it. Pa had made the apple peeler. It was a complicated little machine with wooden wheels and gears and a sharp knife blade attached. Each apple was speared on a sharp prong, and with a few turns of the handle was peeled in a fraction of the time it would take to peel it by hand. Then that apple was placed in a bowl and when the bowl was filled, it was shoved along to the next girl in line. She halved and quartered them, the next one to her cored them and took out any bruised spots. Two girls were kept busy carrying baskets of apples from the porch, and Mary, who was a little young to work with a sharp paring knife, emptied the pails of peels and cores into a big tub for Delcy. The wooden wash tubs and the copper wash boiler were lined with clean white cloth and the apples were piled in and covered.

"They're beginning to get brown already," Mary noticed after a few layers of cut apples were in the tub.

"Can't help a little browning," Ma answered placidly. "They'll be plenty dark before they're through, anyway. But keep them covered as much as you can. The more moisture, the better the sauce."

They sang as they worked, "Blue Tail Fly" and "Charlie is My Darlin' " and all the rest of their favorites, verse after verse. It made the work go faster. Every few minutes they changed jobs so that no one would get bored and sleepy and careless with the knives. Even so, the job was a long one.

"I never want to see another apple again," Hettie

yawned. "We must have cut up a million. I'm almost sorry this was such a good year for apples —" She stopped quickly as she saw Ma's shocked expression. "Well, now, you know I didn't really mean that," she amended her statement. "I'm grateful that we had such a huge crop. It's just that —"

"I know," Ma said. "Apples, apples, apples, for days now. But don't forget, they didn't cost us one precious penny — nothing but a little hard work and that's nothing new. Even the cider pressing was free, thanks to our old miller."

He had refused pay for pressing the Scoville apples, saying gruffly that he guessed he had a right to do a favor for a family he had known for three generations. He finally suggested that a jar of Ma's apple butter would be an acceptable gift for his wife, seeing as his old lady was especially partial to the Scoville recipe.

Mary was her usual practical self.

"Everything else — almost everything else, anyway — we had to plant and weed and hoe and then harvest, and the apples did everything all by themselves, except for picking."

"And next year may be a lean year in the orchard. Apples run like that, you know," Ma reminded them. "Anyway, we're at the bottom of the last basket, so cheer up, Hettie. We're almost through."

And now it was morning before it had really finished being night. The very minute breakfast was out of the way, Ma hurried out to build the fire for the cook-pot.

The best and safest place was in the lane between the yard and the barn where the dried grass of the clearing could not possibly catch fire. Hettie and Sarah and Amanda carried firewood to pile nearby, great chunks of hard wood that would burn slowly and evenly. They would start with a high fire to get the kettle of cider boiling. Later in the process the fire must be slow and even or the apple butter would scorch, and all their days of labor would be wasted.

The huge caldron was made of copper. It had been brought down from its hook in the barn days before and polished inside with salt and vinegar until it shone as brightly as the sun that was now climbing the sky. Ma made a neat ring of stones to hold the kettle up above the fire, and then she and Sarah and Hettie lifted it in place.

"Why is it always a copper kettle Ma?" Amanda asked. "Julia was polishing their copper kettle last week, and Mrs. Hadley had hers out in the back yard cleaning it up."

"Iron would turn the apple juice black, that's why. You'd have the blackest, ugliest looking apple butter — ugh!"

"Ugh!" echoed Mary. "Imagine black apple butter on nice white bread. I couldn't stand it."

When the fire was roaring they poured in pails of cider, and as soon as the first bubbles formed around the edge, the stirring began. Ma took her turn first to set the rhythm and show the others how it must be done, and from that moment on the long wooden stirrer moved constantly. When Ma's arms tired Sarah was ready to grasp the pole and continue the steady even motion without a break. And so it would go all through the day, with Ma and the girls working longer or shorter periods according to their strength.

As the cider cooked down and thickened more was poured in, and the stirrer moved through the center of the steaming brew, around one side, back through the center and down the other side. The pole was longer than Ma was tall so that the person stirring did not have to stand too close to the hot fire. Attached to the end of it was a paddle with holes bored through it, that acted as a sieve and masher when the cut apples were added.

There was a holiday atmosphere about the whole business, even though it was a long and monotonous job. The housework and the outside chores were done for the day and they were free of the usual routine. They all brought stools to sit on between turns at stirring. Ma had her never-empty work basket at hand, Sarah sketched, Teen and Toon and Emily played with their precious stuffed dolls and Mary and Amanda and Nan listened to the stories that Ma could tell so well. She was in the midst of an anecdote about her childhood when they heard a shout from the road. It was little old Mrs. Nixon toiling up the steep mountain lane.

"I knowed it!" she exclaimed as she came closer. "I knowed it when I saw you girls pass yesterday in Moore's wagon with the load of apples. They'll be makin' butter today, I said, and I'm agoin' up there to lend a hand."

From the basket over her arm she whipped out a clean apron and tied it around her waist.

"It's a pleasure to see you, Mrs. Nixon. Don't think about lending a hand. Just sit and visit. Amanda, get the rocker for Mrs. Nixon."

"Now, never mind, Manda. When I'm ready to set, one of them stools'll do fine. In the meantime, let me stir a few strokes. I declare I'm itching to help with a batch of apple butter made proper, and Lord knows my girls don't want help. They know it all without a word from me."

She took the stirrer from Ma and continued without a break in the easy rhythm. "Coming along nicely, ain't it? Soon be ready for the apples. Do you know what that Clara thinks is apple butter? Scorched up applesauce, that's what. Can't abide it."

Clara was one of Mrs. Nixon's five daughters-in-law. Each of the Nixon boys had married and brought his bride home to the big sprawling farmhouse that had housed for so many years a big sprawling family. The Nixon girls had married, too, but they all lived elsewhere, scattered on farms around the valley. Mrs. Nixon sighed.

"Funny how a house is plenty big enough for a family when they're growin' up, but how cramped it gets with six women battlin' for first place in the kitchen. The boys get along fine, but them wives! Well, I can't change 'em any nor teach 'em, neither, so whenever I get a chance I get away for a few hours. Gives them a breather, and me too. Well, look who else needed a change! Old Lop-ears! I seen him follerin' but I thought he'd weary and go back. He's sixteen now, and showin' his years."

Old Lop-ears, the Nixon hound, puffed tiredly up the

hill. He wagged his tail feebly and sank down to rest and be petted. Teen and Toon ran to get him a bowl of milk, and he barked his appreciation with a deep-tongued bay that brought both Betsy and Biteser to the barn door. Betsy had a new batch of kittens and she hurried back to the haymow to hide them deeper in the sweet hay. Biteser, the big tom cat, advanced on the enemy. Hettie laughed as she shooed him away. "Go pick on someone your own age, Biteser. Lop-ears came to visit, not to fight."

Biteser backed up, stiff legged and bristle haired, to watch from the barn door. Lop-ears ignored him with regal dignity and finished his milk.

Mrs. Nixon finally passed the stirrer to Sarah and sat down to "neighbor" as she called it. She had all the news of the valley to relate, and Ma, who rarely went far from the mountain farm, was glad to hear about Eliza's new baby, and Miz Elkins's hat with the flowers that got caught in the rain and how she steamed it over the tea-kettle and ironed it like it was a shirt and by golly, she wore it to the church doin's and it looked like new. Then there was Peter Hebert's young heifer got down with somethin' but Mrs. Hebert tended her all night like a sick child — gave her croup medicine like a baby — and she pulled through and'll make a fine cow yet.

Soon the cider had cooked down enough and it was time to bring apples. It was Amanda's turn to stir. She kept the paddle going up and down and around and up and back, over and over, as the others added pans of the apples they had cut up the night before. As soon as they had cooked to a soft mush, more were added. The fire had been allowed to die down so that no flames leaped up. Just a steady bed of red coals that cooked the apple butter but did not burn it.

"We're planning just to eat a bite out here," Ma apologized as the sun rose overhead to noonday. "The girls'll fix you a plate. We made baked beans yesterday to save cooking today."

Nan and Mary were both pulling on the stirrer now. They wanted to help, and with Ma and Mrs. Nixon keeping a close watch there was no danger that the apple butter would scorch. The older girls hurried to dish out heaping plates of beans from the brown bean pot in the hearth oven. There was crusty bread, too, newly made, and fresh butter. They were all hungry. It had been a long, busy morning. With mugs of milk for the children and strong tea for Ma and Mrs. Nixon — made almost black the way the old lady liked it — it made a fine dinner.

And eating outside was a change, too. Ma had put plenty of salt pork in the beans and Teen and Toon sneaked pieces of pork to Lop-ears who gobbled it down appreciatively.

They couldn't all eat at once. One was always stirring. But they made the turns short so no one had to wait too long. After dinner, when the plates had all been carried back to the kitchen, the younger children lay contentedly on the grass and stared up at the sky. Emily was soon asleep for it was her nap time, but she was comfortable there and Ma decided not to move her.

"Tell us what you see in the clouds, Manda," begged Teen. "You see better things than anyone else."

"Well, there's a big fat cloud up there with a trunk and a tail, and the three little ones behind her are elephant children. Now they're crowding close together because the wind is blowing so hard, and now they're passing the sun . . ."

"Good gracious!" Ma looked up at the sky, too. "A moment ago it was sunny and now look . . . it's clouding over!"

"That wind'll bring rain," said Mrs. Nixon sagely. "Right out of the east, it is, and that means rain for sure and soon, too."

"Fetch the umbrella, quick, Amanda! And my heavy shawl! If a shower comes up now we'll have a real problem on our hands."

Amanda ran to get Pa's old black umbrella. It was so old it was almost green with age, but if handled carefully it shed rain as well as when it was new. It was big enough to shelter even the copper kettle. A little rain in the apple mixture would do no harm, but rain drops hissing on the hot coals would make ashes fly up. Skimming ashes out of the pot was a tedious job.

"We'll be ready if it comes," Ma said, looking anxiously at the sky. All the blue patches had disappeared and the sky was overcast. "Could be the rain will hold off for hours yet. Bring more apples, Hettie. Sarah, you fetch my spice boxes and measures. The nutmeg is all grated and the cinnamon is ground, and it'll soon be time for it."

"Now don't fret," Mrs. Nixon advised. "Just be comfortable and easy. Frettin' wears a body out and it won't hold off the rain nor bring it, neither."

As soon as the last of the apples were cooked soft, the spices were carefully spooned in, and the air, which had been fragrant before, became heavy with the wonderful rich aroma. It took close watching now and a low, low fire. Ma pushed a piece of wood in under the kettle and with the poker shoved back another chunk that was burning too fiercely. It was so important to have it turn out right.

The apple butter was getting hard to stir now. Hettie and Sarah and Amanda stood close by to take over each time Ma's arms tired. Mrs. Nixon sat on her stool and talked, ready with the umbrella as soon as the first drop of rain might fall.

"By the way," she remarked. "I 'most forgot. One of the things I came about was to arrange for you to take over my birthin's."

Ma was so surprised she almost stopped stirring for an instant. Mrs. Nixon was famous in the area as the best "birthing woman" about. When it was time for a baby to be born it was Mrs. Nixon who was called first, and the doctor way over in the next valley only if serious trouble developed. She had the reputation far and wide among the country people of being extremely capable, and families breathed easier when they knew Mrs. Nixon was on her way.

"Yes, you," she continued, although Ma had not said anything. "You're a good nurse, you know it, and heaven knows you've had plenty of experience with your own. I'm not getting any younger and it's high time people started calling someone else in the middle of the night. I'm getting so I need my sleep. You're needed, Sarah Scoville," she said firmly. "I've thought and thought about who'd be the best one to train to take my place and you're it."

"I've never felt it was right to say no when I'm needed." Ma was thoughtful. "And I can't think of who else —"

"There's nobody else. Nobody has my touch except you. I'll teach you all I know of herbs and medicines, but mainly it's the touch. You have to know when to gentle 'em if they're young and scared, and when to holler at them to buck 'em up when the baby's slow in coming —"

"Ssshh!" Ma glanced at the girls who were listening, fascinated. "This isn't fitting conversation for young children."

"Children!" Mrs. Nixon scoffed. "They're young women growed, most of them. High time they understood how things is. How long do you expect to keep 'em sheltered, anyway? Knowin' is growin', I always said, and I always will. There's nothing shameful about a birthing and no need to whisper when a baby is expected, either. I believe in speakin' out, Sarah Scoville, and I'll do it, too. I birthed you and all your young'uns and that gives me some rights. Now, do you tell 'em or do I?"

Ma's cheeks were pink from the heat and exertion but they flushed even pinker. "I will," she said hesitantly.

"Right away, today. No use putting things off. Anyway, that's settled. I'll spread the word that folks are to call on you and I'll stand by if you need me. And you'll charge, too. That'll give you some extra money you can well use."

"Oh, no!" Ma was firm here. "I can't take money for doing the Lord's work."

"Preachers eat, I notice," Mrs. Nixon remarked dryly. "Doing the Lord's work doesn't affect their appetite none, nor their need for shoes, neither. You charge, I tell you. If people can't pay in money they can contribute a nice ham or a side of bacon, and that won't go a'beggin' with all these mouths to feed. No indeed, you let people pay you. In work, even. Won't harm a strong able-bodied man to chop a cord of wood in return for a healthy baby off to a good start. Birthin's not easy work, I warn you, and I find folks value you more if it's not all free. Keep stirrin', Sarah, or your butter'll be no better'n Ern Moore's."

Mrs. Nixon certainly is a strong minded little old lady, bossy as could be, Amanda thought. No wonder she doesn't always get along so well with her daughters-in-law. But she was kind and immensely good hearted and very wise. Amanda thought her plan was a good one. And what could it be that Ma had promised to explain to them?

The sky had been growing darker and darker as they talked. Then they felt the first splash of rain. All social conversation stopped.

"The umbrella, quick!" Ma said. Mrs. Nixon raised

it and held it over the kettle. Sarah tossed the heavy shawl over Ma's head and wrapped it over her shoulders. Hettie picked up sleeping Emily and ran with her into the house.

"You, too, Teen and Toon. Mary and Nan start washing the dinner dishes. The others get shawls and help me here."

Mrs. Nixon had her shawl out of her basket and over her head. The wool was heavy, hand spun and hand woven and it shed rain easily. Nothing but a cloudburst could penetrate the heavy fibers. And this was not to be a cloudburst, only a short hard autumn shower. There was quite a wind, though, and the rain beat in under the umbrella and hissed and sizzled on the hot coals. They all watched for flying ashes, and the minute any settled on the apple butter, Hettie was there with the wooden skimmer to scoop them out.

The apple butter was a rich mahogany red by now, beautiful to see and heavenly beyond words to smell. The gray crocks were washed and waiting on the porch to be filled and then sealed with tallow candle drippings. It would keep all winter in the cool cellar.

The mixture bubbled in the big kettle with a thick lazy plop, plop. Ma tasted it occasionally while someone else was stirring and added a dash more cinnamon or cloves. Finally the wonderful fragrant mush satisfied her and she said briskly, "That's it!"

Hettie and Sarah thrust a stout pole through the kettle handle and one on each side, they lifted it gently from the fire. Pa had constructed a special carrying pole, with pegs that kept the hot kettle centered in the middle so it could not slide to either side and burn the carriers. They grunted as they hoisted it up to their shoulders and shook their heads when Ma wanted to help.

"We're strong as horses," panted Hettie, "and we've got it balanced just right."

They carried it to the porch and set it down with a thump that splashed apple butter to the rim, but fortunately not over it. Ma and Amanda and Mrs. Nixon got to work now, and while the apple butter was still simmering, they ladled it into the stoneware jars and put the lids on. Nan ran through the rain with the sauce pan of candle stubs. After only a short time over the hissing coals the tallow melted, to be poured around the lid of each jar. When it was finished they all sat down and breathed deep sighs of relief. One more big autumn chore out of the way. One more step towards a comfortable, well-fed winter.

"Let's put the kettle out in the rain," Ma suggested wearily. "Tomorrow will be plenty of time to clean it up. I've seen all the apple butter I want to for today."

Mrs. Nixon wrapped her shawl around her and whistled to Lop-ears, who had retreated to the shelter of the house as soon as the rain began.

"Oh, stay for a bite of supper," Ma urged. "You've helped all day. Now let's socialize a little." Old Mrs. Nixon shook her head.

"Hard enough to get up your road by daylight," she

said. "I'd never make it after dark-fall. And Lop-ears'd be no help if a wild-cat came along." She grinned, knowing full well that it had been many years since a wild-cat had been seen on the mountain.

"As soon as the butter's cooled, the girls will drop off a jar on the way to school," Ma promised. That's nice, thought Amanda. It's nice to be able to give away something for a change. Last year the giving was all the other way and now we can pay some of the neighbors back.

There was no need to remind anyone of bedtime that evening. It had been another long, busy day. One by one they yawned and groped their way through the last of the evening chores. It was Amanda who remembered the mysterious something that old Mrs. Nixon had insisted they be told. She stopped at the foot of the stairs and reminded her mother. Ma's cheeks flushed pink again. She seemed hesitant, almost embarrassed. Ma, who was usually so sure of herself! She said "Well —" and then looked helplessly at Sarah. "Some other evening, when we aren't so tired." Sarah shook her head.

"No, Ma, Mrs. Nixon's right. We are almost women grown and it's right that all of us should understand."

"Then you'll have to tell them. I — I can't find the words —" She put down her mending and fled into her bedroom.

Sarah said gently. "Come back and sit down, Amanda and Nan, and you, too, Mary, and I'll explain. What Mrs. Nixon meant was that we're women all alone with Pa gone and no brothers to watch out for us —"

Brothers! thought Amanda. If William and Henry Moore are any examples, we'll manage better without brothers.

Sarah continued, "Girls without menfolks have to be able to take care of themselves and so they have to understand things younger, maybe, than other girls. But it's hard for mothers to explain. They get all fussed — even Ma, and you know she doesn't fuss easily. What she wants you to understand —"

"Understand what, Sarah? Stop beating around the bush and tell us, for heaven's sake!"

"It's about babies," said Sarah, "and where they come from. That story about the stork — it just isn't true. They grow inside a woman, and they have to be born."

"Oh, that!" Mary breathed a sleepy sigh. "Why didn't you say so? We've known about that for *ages*. It's the same with people as with Betsy and Biteser. If *that's* all there is to it, I'm going up to bed."

4

THE POUNDING on the door was like sudden thunder in the quiet night. It echoed through the silent house and shook Amanda out of her sleep with a start. She sat bolt upright, her heart pounding. The thumping continued and a man's voice called urgently,

"Mrs. Scoville, Mrs. Scoville! Hurry!"

Sarah had awakened too and was shaking Hettie.

"Wake up, Hettie, something's happened!" Sarah felt for the stairs in the pitch dark and Amanda crowded after her. If Sarah was brave enough to go down and face the danger, she would go, too. Behind her she could hear Hettie stumbling out of bed and whispering hoarsely, "Where's the lamp? We'll break our necks in the dark!" But she did not light the lamp on the wash stand after she found it. Until they discovered what the pounding was about they felt safer in the darkness. So they scrambled down the stairs as quietly as they could and opened the stair door into the kitchen. There they stood dazed and blinking in the glow from the lamp that Ma had lighted.

Ma was calling in a low voice, "Just a minute. I'll be there in just a minute." She was buttoning her long flannel wrapper over her nightgown, her fingers flying. When the last button was in place she went to the door.

"Wait, Ma," said Hettie. "We don't know who it might be. Who would come up the mountain after dark?"

Before Ma could answer, the knock came again, and the man called, "Please, Mrs. Scoville! It's my wife, and I don't think there's much time —"

"That's who would come. It must be Mr. Warren, and the Warren baby's three weeks earlier than we expected." Ma opened the door and motioned to the agitated young man who stood there.

"I'll be ready shortly," she said, as calmly as if strangers came often in the dead of night. "As soon as I dress and pack my basket. Sit down and rest and I'll be right with you. Don't be worried, now. Everything will be fine. I'll hurry as fast as I can, but remember, first babies are always slower. Does your horse need water?"

"I — I tied him at the foot of the road, ma'am — figured I could come up this trail faster on foot. And I didn't bring my buggy. I was too excited to hitch up, I guess. I just threw a saddle on my horse and came tearing out to tell you. My wife's all alone —"

"If you didn't bring your buggy, there's no need to wait for me, Mr. Warren. Go back to your wife and don't worry. I'll be there long before she needs me."

Mr. Warren bounded for the open door and then turned back to say, "I do thank you kindly, ma'am, for coming out in the night. You're sure you can get there by yourself?"

Ma nodded confidently and he hurried off. They could hear his heavy footsteps as he plunged pell-mell down the steep path.

"Lucky if he doesn't fall, and I'll have him to take care of, too," Ma said. "Not even a lantern, poor addled man."

She smiled at the ring of girls who were staring wide-eyed at all this. Nan was up, too, peeking out of the bedroom door. Mary and the little ones were still sleeping soundly.

"Shall I hitch George to the wagon, Ma?" Hettie asked. Ma was frowning as she thought. Then she shook her head.

"It would take longer to get George and the wagon down to Three Corners than it's worth. I can walk as fast as George can, anyway, now that he's so old and poky. I'll take a lantern and I can be at the Warrens' in an hour if I hurry. First I've got to get dressed, though, and pack my basket. After this I'll have everything ready to go on a minute's notice. Well, don't just stand around, girls. Get back to bed. You'll have to do my chores in the morning, more'n likely."

"But Ma — all that way alone, in the dark —"

"That's how it is when you get to be the birthin' woman."

Ma sounded almost gay about the prospect of a long lonely night walk. Sarah felt differently. She said, in the same firm voice that always brought the younger children into line, "No, Ma. One of us'll go along."

"Now don't be silly, Sarah. We won't waste time arguing. I have a lot to do." As she talked, Ma was going back and forth packing her big covered basket with all the things Mrs. Nixon had told her she might need; clean white rags, washed so often they were soft and fine; little bags of soothing herbs for broths and poultices; her big sewing scissors. She opened a bureau drawer and found some of Emily's diapers and baby clothes, just in case the Warrens were unprepared.

Sarah persisted. "Ma, you listen. I'm going with you, or Hettie."

Amanda was amazed. Ma's word was law, and not to be questioned. If she said she was going alone, she would go alone. But Sarah seemed to think otherwise.

"You'll have that big basket to carry and the lantern, too, and it's not fitting for you to be out —"

"Oh, gracious, Sarah. Sometimes you fuss like an old woman. I could walk from here to Waterton and never meet a soul after sundown."

"Ma —"

"All right," Ma gave in. "But not you or Hettie. You'll be needed with the morning chores and the fire." She thought a minute. "Get dressed, Amanda, fast as you can. Nan and Mary can take care of Delcy if we're not back by morning. And if I have to stay longer than I expect, I can send word back with Amanda. Bring your slate. You'll have time on your hands and you might as well study if you're going to miss school. Hurry now, we should have gotten started before this. Find your clothes and dress down here. Let Mary sleep if she can. Be careful with the lamp, girls, and watch the fire at breakfast time. Don't let Emily cry, Nan. She won't understand if she wakes up and finds me gone. Go ahead with the ironing, but mind the irons — don't scorch your petticoats."

Amanda hurried upstairs. Her eyes were accustomed to the dark now and she could see the hump that was Mary silhouetted faintly against the window. She felt for her clothes, piled neatly at the foot of the bed and was into them in a flash. She would do her buttons downstairs. She picked up her stockings and shoes and went down again, laughing to herself at the thought of Mary. Mary would be furious when she awakened and found she had missed all this excitement.

Sarah buttoned Amanda's dress while she pulled on her stockings and buttoned her shoes.

"Your hair looks like a rat's nest," Sarah muttered, "but if you take time to fix it, Ma'll go off without you."

Hettie was on the porch, filling the barn lantern. Nan wanted to help, too, but everything was taken care of. Suddenly she thought of something. She stood on tiptoe to reach into the cookie crock and brought out a handful of molasses cookies. Wrapped in a neat bundle, they fitted into Amanda's pinafore pocket.

"You may get hungry on the trip, or maybe there won't be much for breakfast," said Nan sleepily.

Ma was ready now, and much neater than Amanda. Her long thick braids were brushed and pinned up around her head and she was as wide awake as if it were their regular getting-up time. She kissed everyone goodby, quickly and efficiently, and motioned to Amanda to carry the basket. She picked up the lantern and started out. At the door she hesitated, and for a moment she seemed as young and timid as Nan.

"Take care, girls. Bar the door as soon as we're out."

The door was never barred except against the push of the wind in winter, for they always felt completely safe in the mountain farmhouse. Ma's caution made their leaving somehow solemn. Sarah and Hettie and Nan nodded and waved goodbye without a word as Ma and Amanda stepped out into the darkness.

Everything had happened so fast that Amanda still felt a little dazed. First the pounding on the door, and then in no time at all they were on their way. It was all so surprising she could hardly believe it. But she was glad she had been chosen to go. It was another adventure, and there was nothing Amanda Jane Scoville enjoyed more than an adventure.

She and Ma said little as they picked their way cautiously down the rocky rutted lane. The lantern cast a bright light on the road, making everything else seem blacker by comparison. Once Ma said, "We really must work on this road before winter. It's getting so we can hardly get in or out, and we should get some of these rocks cleared out before snowfall. But there's never enough time —"

They were concentrating too hard on keeping their footing to waste time on conversation, and they went along slowly. Once at the foot of the hill, at Three

Corners, they were on smoother ground. They moved along at a brisk pace, Ma walking with long steady strides and Amanda keeping up with an occasional skip to bring her in step again.

Ma seemed lost in her own thoughts. Probably trying to remember all the things Mrs. Nixon had been teaching her in their recent sessions together. Ma had laughed about her "school." When the older girls were off to the schoolhouse in the valley and the little ones were playing contentedly with their dolls, Mrs. Nixon and Ma talked. Or rather, Mrs. Nixon talked and Ma listened and soaked in all she could of the old lady's store of wisdom. Mrs. Nixon knew so much, all the lore of the garden herbs and the wild things that grew in the woods. Some of it had been told to her mother by an Indian woman, and that was a long time ago. Mrs. Nixon said the Indians knew a lot of things that the up-to-date doctors hadn't even begun to guess, and in a pinch she'd bank on the Indians.

"Not that Doctor Harlow isn't a good man," she always added. "Fair's fair, and I have to admit he won't spare himself none. Goes day and night, he does, and never turns down a call, even when he had to drive hours to get there. But just the same, even he turns to wintergreen oil for a chest cold. And it was the Indians who showed the first settlers where the wintergreen growed and what it was good for, besides somethin' nice to chew on."

Mrs. Nixon came up often to give Ma a lesson. At last she said, "You'll do, Sarah Scoville. Next time I'm asked to come, I'm sending you. You know everything I do, almost, and the rest'll come with practice and time."

This was the time, and the pounding on the door and the hurried trip would be part of their life from now on. Amanda was pleased to be chosen to go with Ma. Pleased, and curious, too. She didn't remember Nan's or Mary's birth, but when Teen and Toon were born she was farmed out to Julia's for the day. She came home to find Ma in bed, pale and tired and happy-looking, with two red faced fuzzy-headed babies beside her. Emily came suddenly in the night, and all the children had been banished to the upstairs room to huddle together and listen fearfully to the sounds from below. Now she would be right there, and maybe Ma would ask her to help.

They walked along in silence, past the darkened houses of people they knew well. In the daylight the doors and windows would be open. There would be a wave from someone at the back door or a shout from the barn as they passed. But the houses were as deeply asleep as their occupants, with eyelids lowered and no sign of recognition.

The tall trees on either side of the road rustled in the slight breeze, and Amanda pulled her shawl closer around her shoulders. A cool mist rose from the road and when it dipped down into a hollow, they walked, wraith-like, through drifting fog. The beam of light from the lantern shone dimly against the night that moved around them. Occasionally the light caught a pair of glowing eyes watching from a low thicket, or from a tree branch that overhung the road. Amanda knew that it was only a rabbit or a raccoon but she stuck close to Ma just the same. She was glad she didn't have to go along here in the dark alone.

The road turned out across the flat open pasture land of the valley, and it was much lighter there. They could look back and see the black bulk of their mountain behind them. Above it, the sky was cloudless and clear. Ma spoke for the first time,

"I think we can blow the lantern out now. There's plenty of light to travel by. No use wasting good oil."

"Is it coming morning?"

"False dawn, I'd guess. It won't be really morning for a couple of hours yet. Did you notice the time when we left?"

Amanda had to admit that she had been in too much of a rush to glance at the clock. "I wasn't thinking about what time it was — just about dressing fast. Do you suppose we'll be there quick enough? Should we run a little?"

"I don't think so." Ma sounded sure of herself, unworried. "These things take awhile, you know." Amanda didn't know, and wished she did. Whenever Betsy had kittens it was all over so quickly and easily, and no one had to come to help. She had always known exactly what to do, even with her very first litter. It was different with people, but how different?

"Mr. Warren was in an awful sweat —"

"Prospective fathers always are. I remember how your Pa carried on. That'll be your job, Amanda. Keep George Warren busy and out from underfoot."

Amanda had hoped to be allowed to help with the important part of birthing. What on earth could she do to keep Mr. Warren out from underfoot? She wished Ma would be more specific, but Ma only said,

"We'll be there soon. As I remember, the Warren place is right on the main road, and it should be lighted up."

She was right. Across a small bridge and around the turn and there stood the one house in the valley that was blazing with light. A lantern was glowing at the roadside to mark the path. Ma called softly to warn the Warrens of their approach, but not so loud as to startle them. At the first sound Mr. Warren came charging out to meet them.

"Thank heaven you're here! I thought something had happened to you. Hurry, hurry!"

He urged them into the house and pointed to the bedroom door. He started to follow Ma in, but she stood in the doorway and barred his path.

"Now that I'm here, Mr. Warren, you must remember that I'm in charge."

"But it's my wife," he argued, "and my baby —"

"Nevertheless, you must do just as I say." Ma was kind but firm. "I'll call you when I need you."

This had been Mrs. Nixon's first lesson. Ma was amused at the time, but Mrs. Nixon insisted, "No, I'm not joking. The first thing you've got to do when you go in is let 'em know who's boss, and from then on they all do whatever you need done."

So Ma was following Mrs. Nixon's directions, and it

seemed to work. Mr. Warren stopped blustering and turned back from the bedroom door, meek as could be. He ran his hand through his hair, which was already going every which way, and he hurried over to fling another log on the fireplace. The room was stifling hot. Amanda took off her shawl and moved as far as she could from the blaze. Mr. Warren paced up and down and didn't seem to notice that she was there. She felt like an intruder, but she didn't know what to do about it. Perhaps it would be best to engage him in a conversation to take his mind off his worries. But what would she say? Especially when he hadn't as much as nodded at her.

She sat on a low stool in the corner and looked around the room. It was a nice-sized house and newly built. Not many things in it yet, but what there was was neat and clean. Evidently young Mrs. Warren was a good housekeeper.

Amanda wished she had her slate, but it was in Ma's basket. At least she could draw on it to amuse herself and keep awake. The heat from the fireplace could be felt clear across the room and she was getting sleepy. Mr. Warren poked nervously at the fire and put in another log. Amanda had just decided that she would tiptoe to the bedroom door and ask Ma for her slate when a low moan from inside stopped her. It stopped Mr. Warren, too. He turned white as a sheet and reached for the woodpile. To her surprise, Amanda found herself saying in a firm voice very like Ma's,

"That's a waste of good firewood, Mr. Warren. You'll set the roof afire if you make it any hotter."

Mr. Warren turned and looked at her. He was surprised, too. She had been sitting so quietly that he had forgotten she was there at all.

"You're right, I guess. But what *can* I do?"

Ma had said that her job would be to keep Mr. Warren busy and out from underfoot. Poor worried man, she really felt sorry for him. But it was too early and too dark for barn chores. What could he do? She looked around the room. Everything was neat as a pin. Then she noticed that the supper dishes were on the cupboard, still unwashed. Only a few, two plates and two cups and knives and forks, but maybe she could stretch it out.

"I'll do the dishes, Mr. Warren. I'll need water. Will you get me some?"

There was a pail of water right there, but the distraught man didn't notice it. He grabbed a bucket and hurried out. In a minute she heard the creak, creak, creak of the well rope, and he came bounding in again. Oh dear, why did he have to be in such a hurry. She could see that keeping him busy was going to be quite a problem.

The teakettle hanging over the fire had long ago boiled dry. In fact, with the flames licking around it, it was a wonder it hadn't melted completely. Mr. Warren stayed occupied for awhile just with lifting the hot kettle from the crane with a pair of fire tongs, all the while explaining that the first thing he wanted to get for his wife was an iron cooking stove. Amanda could sympathize with this. She had been impressed with the stoves she had seen on her summer travels, and was even planning that next year's sewing machines sales might bring in enough money to buy one.

The hot kettle had to cool a little before they dared fill it with cold water, and then there was another wait while the water boiled and Mr. Warren tried to remember where his wife hung the dishpan. All in all, Amanda was able to stretch a few dishes into quite a job, and Mr. Warren was distracted from the serious business going on in the bedroom. But there was a limit to the time one could spend on such a small task. Then there was Mr. Warren, worried and underfoot again. He watched the clock as he paced up and down.

"What's happening?" he demanded to know. "Does it always take so long?"

"I don't know, Mr. Warren," she confessed. "This is the first baby Ma's ever birthed, and I just don't know —"

As soon as she said it she realized that this was one time when absolute honesty was not the best policy. A little beating about the bush would have been better.

"The first baby!" he roared. "The first baby, and it had to be mine! Mrs. Nixon let me think that your mother knew all about it — why, *anything* could be going on in there with a fuddling bumbler."

Amanda had felt sorry for the anxious young man before, but now she was angry. All the manners that Ma had taught her flew right out of her head. She stood in front of him, hands on her hips, face as red as a rooster's, and said,

"Don't you dare call my mother a fuddling bumbler

— or anything else, either! If Mrs. Nixon thought she was ready to go out birthing babies, then she is! Be glad she was willing to come all this way in the dark to help your wife — a fine job you'd have made of it, all alone."

A sudden loud wail from the bedroom interrupted them. They both stood stock still and listened. There was no doubt, it was a new baby's cry. Amanda and Mr. Warren forgot their angry exchange of words and turned to the doorway. In a minute, there was Ma, smiling.

"You have a son, Mr. Warren. A nice strong boy. And Mrs. Warren is fine, just a little tired. In a little while you may come in to see them. Amanda, will you hold this blanket by the fire to warm it and then give me a hand?"

Amanda took the little scrap of soft blanket and warmed it before the fire that had died down to a pleasant glow, and then hustled in to help. Ma was cleaning a squalling little red creature with a soft cloth. She wrapped him in a flannel binder and then in the warmed blanket.

"We'll dress him up later," whispered Ma, "but for now he just needs to holler a little and rest." She handed the baby to Mrs. Warren to hold, and flipped the coverlet over the bed, smoothing it neatly. "Now Mr. Warren, come in."

He stumbled into the room, and Amanda found that she was neither angry at him nor sorry for him. He was dog-tired and rumpled, but his face, as he looked at his pretty, weary wife and new little son, was so proud and happy that Amanda couldn't be anything but pleased. Ma motioned to her to leave and they tiptoed out. Ma sank down onto a stool and sighed,

"Well, that's done. Our first birthing, Amanda, and we did it all right. How did you manage with Mr. Warren? It was a long night."

Amanda noticed with surprise that it was daylight. The first early rays of the sun were coming in the window. She started to tell Ma that she had flared up at Mr. Warren, but it no longer seemed important. He had been upset and so had she.

"We crossed swords," she said primly, "but the least said, soonest mended." This was a direct quotation from Ma, and her mother laughed.

"Anyway, I kept him occupied, the way you said. We washed dishes half the night, same two plates over and over. I don't know what I'd have done if Mrs. Warren had had time to do the supper dishes. Next time I'll bring a few dirty dishes with me, just in case."

She looked sidewise at Ma as she said this, to see how Ma felt about bringing her along on all her birthing cases. Ma didn't miss the hint.

"Oh, Amanda Jane, whatever will I do with you? You'll use any excuse to be up and traveling, won't you?"

Ma didn't say yes to the unspoken question, but neither did she say no. It was as close as she would come to a direct answer, Amanda knew, so she let the matter drop. But she resolved to be ready when the next time came. At the first knock at the door she'd be dressed and downstairs in a flash, and she'd have a basket packed, too.

"We'll get breakfast," Ma continued. "I'm starved, and I'll bet everyone else is. I'll stay here for awhile yet. Mr. Warren has arranged for a neighbor girl to come in and help, but I want to wait around and get everything going right. You can take the lantern and go home. Tell them I'll be along later."

Ma found where Mrs. Warren kept everything. In a few minutes the house was filled with the wonderful fragrance of boiling coffee and frying bacon. There was a cow lowing from the barn as Mr. Warren came out of the bedroom in answer to Ma's soft call.

"She's asleep," he whispered happily. "They're both sound asleep. I don't know how to thank you, Mrs. Scoville."

"Don't even try," said Ma. "Eat your breakfast, now, and then you've got chores to do. The cow's calling to be milked — no —," she stopped him, "Don't go out now. The cow will wait and your stomach can't. Eat while it's hot and good."

And he did. His long night of pacing and worrying had given him an enormous appetite. He ate stack after stack of pancakes. Amanda was amazed that one person could hold so much. When he was finally finished, he said bashfully,

"I'm meaning to pay you, ma'am, for all you've done. But I was thinking just money alone doesn't seem enough — like just buying something at the store. I'd like to *do* something, sort of in little Joshua's name."

He hesitated and then said all in a rush, "That road of yours, ma'am. I never traveled any rockier, and I kept thinking, what if I break a leg and don't get back to my wife in time. If it won't hurt your feelings, may I work on it a little when I have free time, for the next fellow who has to come in the night?"

Amanda took her time going home. If she didn't hurry too much she could make it just in time to let Sarah and Hettie and Mary and Nan go to school while she stayed home with the little ones. She felt like having a day off from school. She was wide awake now but later on she would need a nap.

She scuffed along in the dust, swinging the unlighted lantern, enjoying the autumn sunshine. The road wound and dipped across the valley, bright and sunny, with no secret shining eyes or ghostly patches of mist. A few heads of Queen Anne's Lace clustered by the roadside, and some wild asters were host to a big bumblebee, out for the last nectar of the season. A late katy-did sang from the wild rose thickets and Amanda sang too, a song that seemed to fit in with her feeling of happiness about the new day and the new baby.

I gave my love a ring that had no end,
I gave my love a baby with no cry-en.

She laughed at that part. Little Joshua Warren hadn't been a baby with no cry-en, that was certain. Little Josh was a squaller. Well, good for him. You have to be able to speak up when it's necessary, she decided. She did, too often, maybe. She stayed out of trouble more by good luck than good management. This thought didn't dim her high spirits one bit. She went on with her song, louder than ever,

"A baby when it's sleeping is no cry-en."

5

THERE WAS A WHIP to the autumn wind. It pushed and pulled at the Scoville girls as if it were hurrying them about their fall chores. The scarlet and gold leaves swirled in eddies around the clearing and came to rest against the house, only to be picked up and blown on by the next impatient gust.

Amanda came in from the spring with a pail of water and stood panting, with her back to the kitchen door to keep it closed. Her hair was mussed and her cheeks were as red as the falling leaves.

"I'll bet we have frost tonight," she predicted breathlessly. "It's getting downright chilly."

"Then let's pick the last of the zinnias," Ma said. "It breaks my heart to see them all blackened and withered with frost when we could have the pleasure of them inside for a few more days. And any tomatoes, too, red or green. We can always ripen the green ones on the windowsill or make a crock of green tomato pickles — get down from that cupboard, Teen, you'll break your neck — or tomato relish."

Ma's conversation was often like this — broken into bits that all ran together into one sentence. But with three lively ones like Teen and Toon and Emily underfoot and into mischief it was unavoidable. Teen climbed reluctantly from the stool she had pulled up, intending to investigate the higher shelves of the big cupboard.

"Here, all of you wrap up warm and go with Amanda to pick tomatoes. For once it doesn't matter if you know green from ripe. Just bring me all you can find."

"I don't want to pick into Manda's basket," said Toon. "I want a basket of my very own."

"Me too," said Teen, and Emily echoed, "Me too."

"Good heavens," cried Ma in despair. "Are we going to have *another* Me Too? Why can't all of you use Amanda's big basket and then you won't have to carry it?"

"I need a real basket of my very own," Teen insisted and this time it was Toon who said "Me too." Emily piped, "My own basket. I *need* my own basket."

Ma sighed and then smiled. "I guess when you're big enough to do a grown up job like picking tomatoes, you do need your very own basket. Wait a minute." She stood on a stool and reaching up to the ceiling beams where baskets of all sizes and shapes hung, and brought down three small ones.

"We've got to hurry. Frost'll be here any minute. Come on, you slow pokes." Teen herded the others through the door and bustled importantly out to the vegetable garden. Ma and Amanda had to laugh at the three of them, as full of business as three old ladies, racing to get ahead of the frost that could not possibly come until the middle of the night.

"I'll let them do the tomatoes," Amanda said. "It makes them feel so biggetty, and there aren't many, not enough to keep us all busy. I'll pick flowers. It's more fun, anyway."

"Don't cut the chrysanthemums," Ma called after her. "They don't mind frost, and they'll give us some color later on."

Amanda gathered an armload of brilliant zinnias. They seemed to grow with an extravagant burst of energy in the sun of mid-autumn, as if they knew their days were numbered and each one must count for two. There was something sad about them in spite of the gypsy color. They gave her the same lonesome chill down her spine that she got when she smelled the blue smoke of burning leaves, or when Ma sang one of the old, old songs of unhappy love that her people had brought over from Scotland a hundred years before. It was strange how you could be sad and happy at the same time. She didn't know why, but she knew for certain that it was true.

She loved the autumn, for all its undertones of sadness. There was an excitement in the wind and the snappy air and in the wild swirl of leaves. Even the wet days were rich with color, the rain dripping from leaves darkened to a deep wine red. And the mists and fogs that circled the mountain early in the morning, shutting them off from the rest of the world. There was a kind of excitement in that, too.

The last of the katydids, now singing katy-don't, katy-don't, and ending on a lower tone than their summer song, would soon be over, gone with the frost. She would miss them both, the cicadas who buzzed in the day, and the katydids who took up their unmusical shouting each evening, bless their little dried-up hearts!

She could hear Teen and Toon squabbling in the garden, and once Emily fell and whimpered. Amanda stopped picking flowers to listen. If Emily set up a howl she would run to help her, but if it was just an ordinary tumble Emily would struggle to her feet and stagger on with no help needed or wanted. Apparently this was the case now, for in a minute Amanda heard her brag, "I found a *big* one, part red and part green." So she was all right.

Amanda made three trips to the house before all the zinnias were picked. They overflowed the big brown crock into smaller jars for the table and windowsill.

"Pick off all the leaves that will be under water," Ma cautioned her. "Nothing in the world smells so putrid as zinnia leaves when they begin to spoil." There certainly was nothing putrid about the smell in the little house. Ma had set bread to rise the night before and now it was baking in the brick oven at the side of the fireplace. Loaf after loaf of it, brown and crusty and fragrant. The heavenly yeasty odor made Amanda think of the full flour barrels, full of their own coarsely ground flour — security and plenty for the winter to come. Mixed with the smell of baking was the spicy brew that Ma was simmering in a small kettle hanging from the crane. Vinegar and honey and spices to make relish from the green tomatoes the little girls were still picking.

"We won't bother to preserve the tomatoes for later," Ma said. "We've got shelves of pickle-stuff. I'll make this up and we'll eat it fresh. It'll go down well with baked squash and new bread tonight."

It would indeed. Amanda was beginning to feel hungry already and the morning was only half over. Mary and Nan had gone up into the woods to look over the nut situation.

"Just looking," Mary explained. "We'll find the best trees and then we can all go back with sacks when they're ripe." This was only an excuse to escape to the woods for the morning and get out of housework, and Ma knew it as well as Amanda did. All of them knew the location of every good nut tree on the mountain top, black walnuts and hickory and butternuts, and sweet mealy chestnuts to roast in the embers on chilly evenings. But this was one of those rare Saturday mornings when chores were few in contrast to the busy weeks they had spent harvesting and storing and preserving for the winter. And today was such a beautiful day that Ma had said,

"Go ahead, then, if you like. Find the nut trees for us and we'll pick them after frost."

Mary and Nan had packed a lunch and planned to stay out all day. Knowing Mary, Amanda was sure that the lunch would be eaten by midmorning and that they would be home long before supper. Sarah and Hettie were in the barn, Hettie grooming her beloved Royal

George while Sarah oiled and polished his harness and played with the kittens. It was a nice kind of day, a break in the routine of school and home duties. Amanda thought that after dinner maybe she'd walk down and visit with Julia if Ma didn't need her, or better yet, just sit under the big maple all alone and look over the valley and think about things. It had been a long time since she had had leisure for that.

She brought in a bunch of Queen Anne's Lace and Farewell to Summer for good measure. They were not garden flowers but grew everywhere. They were pretty, though, and Ma liked the wild things as well as the cultivated ones. Once in a while the wind caught the sound of Bossy's big cowbell and the tinkle of the smaller bell around Belva's neck. Belva Belvedere was the calf's name, a fine fancy name for a creature who would someday be a fine fancy cow. Then wouldn't they have the quantities of milk and butter, and plenty left over for puddings and cottage cheese.

Amanda recalled what Mr. Aaron had told her about life in cities. Every drop of milk or cream had to be bought, and if you wanted a flower to brighten the house you *paid* for it. She guessed her bunches of roadside weeds, even, would be treasured in the city. Imagine not being able to pick a flower! She thought about it and decided that Mr. Aaron must have been stretching the truth a mite. Or else they were richer up here on the mountain than ever they had dreamed. There was always something bright to pick and bring inside. Clusters of orange bittersweet when the flowers were gone, and branches of pine with cones on them in winter. And the clumps of parsley and chives that Ma kept growing almost until spring in spite of the cold outside.

Amanda was right about the frost. As soon as the sun started to go down it was noticeably chilly, and by night there was a real nip in the air. The next morning the zinnia stalks stood twisted and blackened. Amanda was glad all over again for the color that blazed indoors. If she changed the water the flowers would stay nice for days yet.

There was a week or so of nippy cold taste-of-winter weather when the squirrels and the chipmunks scurried frantically and the last of summer's songbirds packed up and flew away. Then the capricious weather switched again, and there came a spell of warm langorous days when the wind stopped blowing and the sun hung like a golden disk in the cloudless sky. There was a blue haze at the horizon that Ma said was the Great Spirit of the Indians smoking his pipe. Since Wahkonda was the ruler of the world, he could command the winds to cease blowing until he had finished smoking his pipe. And the wind stopped blowing. There were no clouds in the sky for there was no wind to bring them. There was no wind to carry away the smoke and so it drifted over the valleys and forests in a blue haze.

Then when the Great Spirit had composed his thoughts and finished his smoke, he emptied out his pipe and the north wind broke loose and howled down from the hills, warning all the wild things to make ready for the winter that was coming.

"And so that time of windless calm and blue haze is called the Indian Summer," Ma finished her story.

"You don't believe it, do you, Ma? That old Indian Story?' Hettie asked. They were all gathered around the table, doing their lessons. Ma, as always, was mending.

"I don't know why not," she answered, holding a stocking heel up to the light. "The Indians knew a lot of things about weather and medicines and foods that grow in the woods. They were uneducated in our ways, but very wise in their own. And you'll have to admit that the haze is there. Looks exactly like pipe smoke to me."

"But that's — that's *heathen,* Ma to talk about a Great Spirit like that!"

"Heathen, Hettie? I'm not so sure. Maybe it's just a different name for the same idea. Anyway, think what you will, but enjoy the weather. It won't last."

It was on one of those delightful days of Indian Summer that an unexpected visitor came to the mountain farm. Amanda and Mary and Nan had just waved goodbye to Julia and Thomas at Three Corners. As they climbed the mountain lane they heard the sound of a horse's hoofs and the squeak of buggy wheels. They turned to look, for everyone who passed was an object of curiosity. Surprisingly enough, the buggy did not continue on the valley road but turned up the lane after them.

"Is it Uncle Bolivar?" asked Nan fearfully. "Ma said he might be along any day now." None of them looked forward to Uncle Bolivar's visits of inspection. They dreaded the criticism they knew he would deal out, whether or not it was deserved.

Amanda shook her head and peered down the hill through the tree branches.

"Nope. Uncle Bolivar's buggy has black seat cushions and this buggy has red — it's — Oh, it is, it is! It's Mr. O'Leary! Mary, Nan, it's Mr. O'Leary, my artist friend!"

She turned and ran down the hill. The horse was laboring up the steep road and the driver had gotten out to ease the load.

"Mr. O'Leary!"

He held out his arms and she ran right into them. They hugged each other rapturously, both talking at once.

"— So wonderful to see you — Did you paint Mrs. Nickerson — How have you been? — So many times I've thought of our fortunate meeting —"

All at once Amanda realized that her behavior was not what Ma would consider "becoming." After all, she had known this young man for only a few hours. He was a chance acquaintance she and Mr. Aaron had made on their peddling trip, and here she was, acting as if he were a long-lost relative. Suddenly shy, she drew back and said formally,

"Will you be so kind as to come up to the house, Mr. O'Leary, sir? My mother would be pleased to meet you. I've spoken of you."

"And I have spoken of you, my wee friend," the tall young man answered. "Mrs. Nickerson and I did not agree on every subject, but on one we were in perfect accord. Amanda Jane Scoville," he said, imitating Mrs. Nickerson's pompous voice, "is a most unusually well-brought-up child — a real delight. On this we agreed completely. Not only well-brought-up, I said, but the maker of the most heavenly cup of tea as ever passed my lips, and her toasted cheese — !"

Amanda felt shy no longer. It was as if she had known Mr. O'Leary forever. "Do hurry," she urged. "I can't wait for the others to see you. Sarah will be out of her mind with delight. A real artist! She's never met an artist. Will you have time to give her a lesson, do you think?" She tugged at his hand and he tugged at the horse and they struggled up the hill to the place where Nan and Mary stood openmouthed.

"Mary and Nan, this is my good friend, Mr. Padraic O'Leary, the best artist in all the world! This is Nancy Rowanna Isella Carver Scoville, Mr. O'Leary. She has the longest name of us all but no one ever uses it. Ma made it up from a lot of books she liked. And this is Mary Isabella, the next youngest sister. The rest are all at the house, or will be soon. Sarah and Hettie stayed late today to help Master Pulsifer tidy up the schoolhouse."

They walked Mr. O'Leary and his horse and buggy to the top of the hill and left the patient horse to graze while they ushered the artist excitedly into the house. Ma was surprised indeed to find Amanda pulling a complete stranger by the hand. When Amanda announced his name she smiled and shook his hand.

"Do come in, Mr. O'Leary. Amanda and Mr. Aaron

told us about you. We had hoped we would meet you some day. Girls," she said to the younger ones, who were bashful about coming forward, "Mr. O'Leary drew the pretty faces for your lovely dolls." Teen and Toon curtsied and stared, but Emily hid her face in Ma's apron and took quick peeks at the newcomer when she thought he wasn't looking.

Ma and Mr. O'Leary sat down while Amanda made tea and Mary and Nan got cookies from the big cookie jar. All the time she was stirring the fire to bring the teakettle to a boil and getting out the best cups, Amanda could hear Ma asking polite questions, what Ma herself called being "nosey with manners." Good heavens! Amanda thought, this is *Mr. O'Leary!* You'd think he was a highway man or a tramp, the way Ma was pinning him down on where he had been and where he was going. Then she thought, more reasonably, well, what do we know about him, really? Nothing, except that he's a good artist and sings and plays the violin and tells stories — and he's nice, she added fiercely. I just know he's nice. He's a good kind friend.

Ma evidently thought so, too, for as Amanda brought the cups of tea, her straight back relaxed and she leaned back in her rocker and smiled.

"It's a great pleasure to have you, Mr. O'Leary. We're glad you've come."

"And it's glad I am, too," he answered. "I had the pleasure of knowin' your daughter and Mr. Aaron for such a short time, really, that I feared to be presumptuous in stopping by. But that short time was such a pleasant one and made me so remindful of my own family in Ireland and my missin' of them, that I couldn't resist the impulse when I saw my road would pass nearby."

"How long has it been since you've seen your family?" Ma asked sympathetically.

"Four years, ma'am. I left home when I was sixteen to try my wings and make my fortune in the New Land, never for a moment dreamin' I'd be away so long. Well, I've tried my wings, and I can fly, though a little shaky sometimes, but I'm a long way from makin' my fortune."

Four and sixten — Mr. O'Leary was only twenty. With the beard and all, Amanda had thought of him as an older man. He was just out of boyhood, then. No wonder he was homesick for his family. There were quick footsteps on the porch and the door opened. Sarah stood there for a moment framed in the doorway, while she accustomed her sun-dazzled eyes to the dimness of the room. The warm autumn sun shone around her and lighted her auburn hair. For just an instant she seemed to be wearing a red-gold halo. All of a sudden Sarah looked astonishingly beautiful. It was like magic.

Mr. O'Leary seemed dazed as he rose to his feet. He blinked as if the sun was too bright for his eyes. Then Hettie flew in and the door was closed. There were introductions all around and the magic was over. Sarah looked just as she always did, smiling and quiet, and Hettie was Hettie, bubbling with excitement and doing the talking for both of them.

"Mr. O'Leary, the artist! Oh, Sarah, how nice for you! Now he can show you how to use all those paints you've been struggling with. You are going to stay, aren't you, Mr. O'Leary?" She looked at Ma and said, "He is, isn't he, Ma? Oh, say you can, Mr. O'Leary, or we'll all die of disappointment, Sarah especially."

"Mrs. Scoville, ma'am," Mr. O'Leary began earnestly, "I assure you I had no intention of burstin' in and invitin' myself —"

"Nonsense," said Ma. "Of course you'll stay. Hettie's right. We would all die of disappointment if you didn't make us a visit. The only thing," she wrinkled her forehead as she thought, "we haven't a guest room —"

"I've been sleeping in my buggy a good part of the summer, fair weather and foul. The hay loft would be pure luxury. I don't want to be a nuisance at all, at all."

"Will you be comfortable there? It doesn't seem very hospitable to lodge a distinguished visitor in the barn."

"Be easy in your mind, ma'am. Sure there's nothing as cozy as new-mown hay. I'll sleep like a log, I promise you."

"Then stay and welcome. It will be nice to have you. And now, girls, don't stand there gawking. Let's get Mr. O'Leary's guest room fixed up while it's still light. I'll think about supper."

"We'll make the bed, Ma," Amanda offered, "and Mr. O'Leary can give Sarah a drawing lesson before supper — that is," she hesitated, "if you want to, Mr. O'Leary."

Ma said, "We do seem to have taken a lot for granted, Mr. O'Leary. We've just assumed that you're as anxious to teach as Sarah is to learn. I hope we're right, and that it's not an imposition."

He left no doubt at all in their minds that he would be glad to do what he could.

"Mr. Aaron told me of your talent, Sarah, and I promised him that if I ever got this way I would help you. Now, mind, I'm not sayin' that I'm the best artist in God's world, at all, but there are a few things I've learned that maybe I can be passin' along. Will you let me see what you've done and we'll go on from there."

So while Hettie and Amanda and all the little girls ran back and forth to the barn with a feather tick and quilts and a goose down pillow, and Ma started to mix and stir and chop, Sarah and Mr. O'Leary looked over the pile of drawings she brought him. She was shy at first because this was the first time anyone who really knew had seen her work. Her family and the neighbors all admired it extravagantly, but they were hardly experts. Almost anything would look good to them. Here was an expert and what would he think?

Sarah's family and neighbors had been right, evidently. Mr. O'Leary beamed as he turned over sheet after sheet.

"These are good, Sarah, really good. You have a clear eye and a fine sensitive hand about you, and a feel for things that are beautiful and delicate in nature. I'd have been pleased to make this Jack-in-the-Pulpit drawing myself, and that's pure truth. But I see no people. Do you not like humans, then?"

"I love humans, Mr. O'Leary, but I don't have the

knack of drawing them, maybe because they don't sit still the way flowers do."

"Then we'll concentrate on people for awhile, and tomorrow if it stays fair we'll try a little landscape in oil. You'll not find a prettier spot to paint than the valley out there and the blue hills beyond. Now about figures, let me show you —"

They bent earnestly over the paper and didn't even notice that Ma was quietly setting the table around them. Even the little ones tiptoed about their chores, so as not to disturb Sarah's long awaited lesson. Actually they could have shouted and banged and Sarah wouldn't have heard it, so engrossed was she in listening to and remembering every word that Mr. O'Leary said. Finally supper was ready and Ma had to interrupt.

"Can you two take time out to eat, I wonder? Artists may enjoy starving, but the rest of us mortals don't," Ma teased gently.

"I'm so hungry my stomach's growling." That was Mary, frank as always.

"Me too," said Teen and Toon. "Me too," Emily added.

Mr. O'Leary laughed. "Me too. Artists do a lot of starving, ma'am, but it's not from choice. We'll all eat if we have the chance, and it doesn't interfere at all with our work. Doesn't it smell delicious, now? I know where Amanda learned her cooking skill."

Supper was good. Plain but good. There was a big round pan of johnny cake and a dish of sweet butter to spread on it. Vegetables from their garden, squash and carrots and creamed onions, and a great skillet of potatoes fried with crisp slices of salt pork, and three kinds of pickles, and a mound of coleslaw, and to top it all off, pie. Mr. O'Leary did it all justice. It pleased Ma to see him enjoy supper so much, but it was Mary who spoke out.

"Stay long enough, Mr. O'Leary, and Ma'll put some meat on your ribs."

"Mary! That's not a ladylike expression!"

Mr. O'Leary was not offended. "Ribs, is it? Another meal like that and I'll need a new set of buttons on my waistcoat. I'm afraid I ate like a man a long time away from the table, ma'am, and it's not my wish to eat you out of house and home. It's just that it's all so good and so like home. If you'll give me chores to do, I'll work and gladly. Just don't send me off until I've had another such pie."

A shadow crossed Ma's face and then was gone.

"My husband was fond of my pies, Mr. O'Leary. It's — it's nice to have a man's hearty appetite to cater to."

"Faith, if it's appetite you're wantin', I'll do my best. And I'm givin' you fair warnin', my best is prodigious."

"Will you sing for your supper, Mr. O'Leary? That would be a treat for us."

"Sing and fiddle, both, ma'am. I'll just get my fiddle from the buggy — Holy heaven above, it's daft I am! I left my horse and buggy and never gave either a second thought!" He leaped to his feet.

"Don't you worry one bit. Your buggy is in the barn, in case of rain, and your horse is rubbed down and fed and stalled next to Royal George. We fixed his bed when we made yours," Hettie laughed.

"Saints be praised, did ever a man get such service, now? Then I'll be bringin' my fiddle and I'll play you a tune that'll make the washin' up go faster. Don't stir, any of you, until I'm back."

When he came in with his fiddle they were all sitting obediently at the table. He settled himself on a stool by the fire and tuned up his instrument. He began to play a melody, light and lovely and jolly. The music took charge of their feet and hurried them around the room. The table seemed to clear itself, the dishes splashed in and out of the soapy water, the hearth was swept and finally, all out of breath and laughing, Ma and the girls sat down and looked around the orderly room.

"Didn't I tell you the livin' truth?" he asked. "The right tune will make any job go faster. Now, what would you like to hear? Name it and it's yours."

One after another he played all their favorites and many more besides, songs they had never heard before. Happy songs, sad songs, funny songs, long ones, short ones, quiet ones. At last he looked over at little Emily on Ma's lap and started to sing softly, "Lully, lullay, thou tiny little child—" He rocked gently back and forth as he played and Emily swayed with him. Her eyes had been sparkling with excitement, but now they drooped and she leaned against her mother. Ma nodded and stood up and Emily never stirred. Lully, lullay, the fiddle sang, and Mr. O'Leary sang with it. Sarah got up and took Teen and Toon by the hand.

"The lullaby is for you, too," she whispered. "Come, it's hours past your bedtime."

Mr. O'Leary let the music fade softly into silence. Mary started to ask for more but Ma came back into the room and shook her head.

"Mr. O'Leary's had a long day, and so have we and morning will come early. We'll have music again tomorrow night, and we'll look forward to it all day long."

She lighted a lamp for Mr. O'Leary. "Take care as you climb up to the loft. The ladder's steep. I hope you sleep well."

"I'll sleep like a log, I'm sure of it, and thank you. God keep you safe and send you pleasant dreams."

From the bedroom window Amanda could see a dim glow in the hay loft. In a minute or two the light went out. A single bright star hung low in the sky and she wished on it as she always did.

"Star light, star bright —"

"Did you wish for Mr. O'Leary to stay a long, long time? I hope so. You're a better wisher than I am," Mary whispered sleepily.

"It's bad luck to tell your wish," Amanda answered. "Move over, and give me some covers."

6

WHEN THEY got up the next morning they hurried through their dressing faster than ever. Ma wanted breakfast to be especially nice for their visitor. And also the older girls had suddenly realized that in the excitement of the evening before not one of them had even opened a school book. So with everything else, there was some hasty studying to be done.

"I'll hear you say your spelling on the way to school if you'll hear mine," Amanda said, her words muffled in the petticoat she was dropping over her head. And Hettie said, "I don't care. I would have gotten that miserable mental arithmetic wrong even if I had studied. I just can't make it come out right unless I write it down."

She and Sarah were dressed first and hurried to the barn. In a minute or two they came back looking very much puzzled. "The horses have been fed and turned out, and Bossy has been milked and the kittens are lapping milk from their dish —"

"And the pigs are slopped, bad 'cess to the smelly things, I say, but for the life of me I can't find where you might be keepin' your chicken feed nor ever a basket to gather the eggs in."

"Mr. O'Leary!" Ma was amazed. "You've done all this? That was kind of you, indeed, but my goodness, what a way for us to treat a guest."

"While I'm here I'd not like to be havin' women wait on me, and me strong as an ox, and eatin' as much as a team, at that. So lead me to the chicken feed and put a basket in me outstretched hand, and you'll be seein' your new hired man."

Ma protested, but Mr. O'Leary was firm, so Mary went with him to the chicken coop. He called back over his shoulder, " 'Twill give you time for more important matters, ma'am, like pie bakin'."

All through breakfast Ma seemed preoccupied. She said something quietly to Mr. O'Leary and he nodded. She was planning something for there was a look of suppressed excitement about her. After breakfast was over she said,

"Sarah, goodness knows how much longer this spell of lovely weather will last. You'd better have your out-of-doors painting lesson today. You're far enough ahead in your school work to miss a day or so, and anyway, I'm sure Master Pulsifer would agree that painting lessons are educational, too."

Sarah was speechless with delight. A whole day of painting! Ma continued, "I have some errands to do down the road and I'm going to leave Teen and Toon and Emily here. They mustn't disturb the lesson, mind.

Children, you are big enough to play quietly nearby and not get into trouble. Teen and Toon, don't let Emily out of your sight for an instant, and all of you stay away from the spring. I'll be back well before dinner time."

"But where are you going, Ma?" Hettie asked.

"That's for me to know and you to find out, and don't forget that it was curiosity that killed the cat," Ma retorted. "But if my plan works, I'll have a nice surprise for you all by the time you get back from school."

The girls didn't know what to say. Ma hardly went anywhere, and never without the little ones. What on earth could she be up to? It seemed that Mr. O'Leary knew, for there was an extra twinkle in his eyes and little lines of laughter pulled at his mouth although he kept his face solemn and serious. Something was going to happen, but what?

"I want to get an early start," Ma said. "I'll walk down the road with you. Hurry now, let's get the dishes finished and the beds made. No lallygagging this morning."

They left Sarah and Mr. O'Leary settled at the edge of the clearing where an opening through the trees gave them a view out over the sloping pasture and down to the valley below. Mr. O'Leary had explained that they must work fast while the morning light lasted, for by afternoon the same scene would look quite different. Teen and Toon and Emily were playing with their dolls, close enough for Sarah to watch occasionally, but not so near that their chatter would be distracting.

All the way down the hill, Hettie and Amanda and

Nan and Mary tried to pry Ma's secret out of her. But coax as they might, she shook her head and would not tell. Julia and Thomas Perkins were waiting at the Perkins gate and they, too, were surprised to see Mrs. Scoville out so early.

"I'm going to pay a call on your mother, Julia. Good-bye, children, have a good day in school." She went up the path to the Perkins house and left quite a little crowd behind her, all staring.

"Nobody goes calling this early, do they, before the chores are done? Leastwise, your mother never has before. Sometimes Evaline Pettingill runs in to borrow a cup of flour, but not Mrs. Scoville."

There was nothing the Scoville girls could tell Julia for they didn't understand it either. Mystified, they went on down the road to school.

They were even more mystified when, at recess time, they saw Ma come into the schoolyard. She smiled and waved at them but went on into the school to speak to Master Pulsifer. She reappeared in a few minutes, waved again and went on. Whatever she had said to Master Pulsifer had put him in a very good humor, for he wore a slight smile all the rest of the morning. And when Steuben Purcell was more unruly than usual, the teacher only looked at him sternly instead of reaching for the birch rod. After the very last lesson of the day had been heard, Master Pulsifer called the school to order.

"Do all of you have one clean side to your slate? If not, I will wait until you do."

There were a few minutes of scrubbing of slates with damp rags and frantic waving of the slates to get them dry. Then when everyone was quiet and ready to write, Master Pulsifer said,

"Now write this on your slate in your best handwriting.

You are cordially invited to attend a singing party at the schoolhouse tomorrow evening at seven o'clock. All the family is welcome, young and old."

The teacher spoke slowly and spelled out the hard words so the youngest scholars could write it down. Then he said,

"Please show this to your parents as soon as you get home from school. And if you have neighbors with no children, be sure they are told about it too. It should be a very enjoyable evening and we wouldn't want anyone to miss it."

There was a babble of questions. Hands popped up all over the room but Master Pulsifer would give no more information.

"You'll find out when you get here," he said. "Now go on home and study well this evening, for there will be no time for schoolwork tomorrow night."

Amanda was so excited she felt ready to burst. Of course! It was all clear now. Ma's secret had been to have Mr. O'Leary entertain at a singing party. It was a wonderful idea and everyone would enjoy it. Not the least part of her excitement came from the fact that it was her own special Mr. O'Leary who would be the most important person there, and if he was the most important person, she would certainly be the second most important, since she had known him longest. It was a very nice feeling.

Julia had guessed the secret, too. Amanda had told her about their interesting guest, every single detail.

"What will we wear, Amanda? Do we come all dressed up, or wear school clothes or what? I've never been to a singing party."

Amanda had to admit that she never had either. "I guess people will wear best clothes. After all, it is a party. My best dress will be too hot for this warm weather, but I don't care, I'll wear it anyway."

Mr. O'Leary had never seen her best dress, she realized, only her old blue ones that had been lengthened with a border of red. Her best dress was really very pretty, and being an artist, Mr. O'Leary would be sure to notice. She ran up the hill, singing as she went. She could hardly wait.

There was a lot to talk about that afternoon. They pressed their best dresses and blacked their shoes so they would look nice the following evening. Even Emily was excited. Although she wasn't quite sure what was going to happen, she wanted to be part of it. Ma explained her idea as they fixed supper.

"We all had such a good time last night that I found myself wishing we could share it with the Perkinses and the Nixons and all the others. I thought about inviting them here, but we just wouldn't have room for them to stand up, much less sit down. All of a sudden I thought of the schoolhouse. Plenty of room and plenty of seats. I checked with Jeremiah Hancock and for once he didn't think something new was dangerous." Ma stopped and laughed. "I'll admit I came down heavy on the patriotic songs we'll be singing, and skipped the funny songs and the love songs — you know, as head of the School Board he'd never approve of that — but, anyway, he agreed it would be appropriate to hold an entertainment in the schoolhouse as long as all the taxpayers are invited. With the weather as warm as it is we won't need a fire so Mr. Hancock couldn't object that we would be wasting firewood on foolishness. Everyone I asked was tickled to come. We haven't had an entertainment in the neighborhood for ages. We'll each contribute a cake or cookies or a couple of pies so we can have refreshments. It will joggle us all out of our work-a-day rut."

Supper was a happy meal. It had been a long time since they had a man at the table, someone who laughed and joked the way Pa used to. They all laughed so much they hardly had time to eat, and yet every platter was cleared. It was wonderful what Mr. O'Leary did for their appetites. Ma had made pie again, pumpkin this time, and Mr. O'Leary declared it was even better than her apple pie, if that could be possible.

After he had played them through the clearing up, he laid his fiddle aside and said,

"You know, there's been so much merriment that I clean forgot the news that I had to pass on to you, now that's a fact, Amanda. Would you believe it, we've never once discussed the paintin' of the grand portrait of Mrs. Nickerson that set me on the road to fame and fortune, all thanks be to yourself."

They pulled their chairs closer to where Mr. O'Leary sat by the dying fire. Amanda sat on the floor close by his knee and he rested his hand on her smooth brown hair as he talked. He looked around the modest room, lighted dimly by the one lamp on the table.

"Will you look at this room, now? All the beams showin' in the ceiling, and the table and chairs made by hands that loved you, and not so much as a flowered carpet on the floor or a rose on the washin' up bowl —"

Then he had slept in the rose-covered guest room, too, Amanda thought delightedly.

"— but it's friendly and so crowded with love and good things it fills my heart to the brim, fair to spillin' over. Not that Mrs. Nickerson's house was not a kind one, nor friendly, but there was a difference, now. I was a guest in her house, sure enough, but a guest who worked with his hands all the same, and proud woman that she is, she never forgot it. I saw right away that I'd have to grasp the reins tight or she'd run away with the whole business. So I laid it on so thick I had to laugh at meself sometimes. I was the grand successful artist who had painted so much nobility that a judge's wife was a slight comedown. I ordered her about and chose the dress I'd paint her in — 'twas the purple silk, Amanda, the one she would have picked anyway. But I was the one who decided. She wanted to sit and I bade her stand, and she gloried in the bossiness of me for she knew she had met her match. The Judge knew it too and he urged me on, the rascal. It is a good picture, if you'll pardon a bit of braggin'. It shows all her false pride and her wilfulness, and then I sneaked the inside kindness of the woman into her eyes. So there she stands in her silken dress and the bit of flowered carpet showin' at her feet, and her garnet brooch a'sparklin' and a look of goodness with it all."

Sarah sighed. "It sounds so wonderful. To be able to put all that in a picture —"

"You'll be doin' it, too, if you keep on workin' at it, never fear."

"Did Mrs. Nickerson like the portrait?"

"She did, indeed, and the Judge as well. She gave an evening sociable and invited all the better class neighbors and friends for miles around. And there I was, the Queen of the May, with the seat of me only good pants shinin' in the lamplight. You'd have thought I was old Rembrandt himself, come back especially for her party, the way she introduced me around. Faith," he chuckled, "you'd have laughed to see the airs and graces I put on for the occasion. I impressed them all so much that Mrs. Partridge decided she would have a portrait, too, a smaller one, just head and shoulders. And then, believe it if you can, the Purvis sisters, both speakin' at once to give each other courage, came forward and asked to have crayon drawings made. Sure, the day I met Amanda and Mr. Aaron was a lucky one for me. Nothing but good has come of it."

Amanda felt as if her cup of happiness was running

over. Ma asked, "Will you find tomorrow's party a come-down, I wonder? We aren't as elegant as the Nickersons."

He looked over at her and mischief crinkled the corners of his eyes.

"I'm used to the very best, ma'am, but I'll do my best to conceal my disappointment and be gracious to the poor hard-workin' peasants, and that's a promise. If you see me unable to carry on, just come forward with a piece of your pie to buck up my flaggin' spirits. Now shall we sing a little? I've held the floor with my blatherin' long enough. What'll it be?"

Emily loved "Froggie Would A-Wooing Go" so they went through all of that. Amanda put her heart into the song, partly because she liked the rollicking tune and partly because she sang well. She wanted to be sure that Mr. O'Leary noticed. When they had exhausted all their favorites, Ma asked thoughtfully,

"Do you know an old one — it's Scottish, I think, not Irish, and sad as can be. Benarry, my mother called it." She hummed the tune and Mr. O'Leary's fiddle followed softly behind. When they had it worked out, Ma sang in her clear sweet voice and he played a gentle blending harmony.

Amanda hugged herself to keep the shivers from running up her spine, it was so beautiful and sad and scary. She could see the King and the Queen-Mother sitting on the dam-sides of Benarry, and the handsome stranger, and the lovely drowned daughter with the golden hair. When Ma finished, they all sat quietly, unwilling to break the spell the song had cast upon them.

Mr. O'Leary played Emily's bedtime song and another wonderful evening was over. Tomorrow there would be enchantment of a different sort. Everything Mr. O'Leary touched was gilded with enchantment, Amanda thought. As she wished on her star that night she couldn't think of a new wish, only last night's, so she wished it again.

"Let Mr. O'Leary stay forever," she wished earnestly. "I wish he could stay forever and ever."

The next day flashed by in a blur of excitement. Master Pulsifer had to spend as much of his day disciplining as he did teaching because it was hard for everyone to settle down to study with the thought of the evening's entertainment ahead of them. When the school day came to an end Master Pulsifer heaved a sigh of relief and sent them home with a few words about better behavior in the future. No one lingered in the schoolyard or dawdled on the way home. There were chores to do and an early supper, and then the dressing up.

William Moore complained,

"I don't see the sense of all this washing and dressing up just to go back to school and sing." Henry agreed with him.

"Stay home, then," Amanda suggested callously. "The place'll be jammed without you anyway, and there'll be just that much more cake for the rest of us."

William and Henry quickly reversed themselves when they heard about the refreshments.

"Oh, we'll come, but it's just to eat. The rest of it will probably be awful. Whoever heard of a singing party?"

"People who have been out in the world have,"

Amanda said in her most superior voice. "If you ever have the opportunity to do any traveling, as I have, there will be many things you'll hear about."

Henry was unimpressed. "Hoity-toity," he remarked. "We'll come, all right, for the eating. But you won't catch us singing. Not us or any of the other fellows."

The Moore boys turned in at their gate, and as the rest of them went up the road Julia asked nervously, "Do you suppose they mean it? What if all the men and boys just come to eat and won't sing? It'll be terrible."

Mary refused to worry. "They'll sing," she said. "Ma said we'd sing first and then eat, and if the women are passing out the refreshments the men-folks will sing or the cake will be passed in the other direction. There's more than one way to skin a cat."

"Besides, Julia," said Nan. "You haven't heard Mr. O'Leary play. When he tucks his fiddle under his chin and plays, you just have to sing along, even if you haven't any more voice than a bullfrog. You can't help yourself."

After a quick supper that night they all got ready for the party. There hadn't been too much question about what to wear. They had one best dress apiece and were glad of it. Sarah was the only one who was wearing her best dress for the first time. She had shot up so tall during her fifteenth summer that nothing would fit her. So early in the fall, before school began, Ma had looked through the hand-me-down chest to see what could be made over. There wasn't much choice. Most of the dresses were Sarah's or Hettie's old ones, ready to be shortened for the younger children. There was one, though, a poplin in a particularly unpleasant shade of yellow-green. It had been Cousin Polly Martin's, and even when it was new it was a horror. When Cousin Polly brought it, Hettie was so outraged that she had wanted to use it for a scarecrow. "It's insulting!" she sputtered. "NO one — no one could wear a color like that! It looks like —"

"No need to be vulgar, Hettie," Ma said mildly. "We all know what the color looks like. But let's not get too big for our britches. The poplin's good quality." So they had kept it, and now Ma had the dress out and was looking at it thoughtfully.

"There are yards of cloth in the skirt alone, and fortunately, the color's not fast. You can see where it has faded."

Toon asked curiously, as she fingered the folds of the skirt, "What is it when the color's not fast?"

"That means it will run, goosey," answered Mary, who always knew everything.

"But if it is fast, it should be able to run. What if the color is slow, will it run then? And does the dress run, too, or just the color?"

Even Hettie had to stop fuming to laugh at this. Ma explained,

"Oh, Toon, it's just a way of saying that the color will wash out of the cloth. Usually we want color to be fast so it will stay pretty and bright and not fade, but this green —" Ma shuddered. "I don't believe in being clothes-proud, but there's no reason why we shouldn't fix this up a little if we can."

They had ripped out all the seams with Ma's tiny embroidery scissors and then they scrubbed each piece of cloth and laid it out on the grass in the bright sunlight to dry. Sure enough, the ugly green faded away to a soft color, a misty gray green that was really pretty. It was streaky in places, but there was so much material that with careful planning Ma could cut around the streaks. There was one darker spot in back. Ma covered it with a soft fall of pleated ruffle that matched the ruffle at the bottom of the skirt. The bodice fitted plain and smooth and the skirt belled out gracefully. No one would ever have guessed that it had once belonged to Cousin Polly, not even Cousin Polly herself.

Sarah was the last one to get dressed. Hettie had buttoned the row of tiny buttons down the back and adjusted the ruffle while everyone else fidgeted excitedly downstairs. At last they came down the steps, Sarah walking carefully so as not to trip on the ruffle and Hettie behind her carrying the lamp. Sarah's red hair glowed in the lamplight and once again she seemed to be wearing a radiant golden halo.

Amanda heard Mr. O'Leary catch his breath in a quick gasp. She turned, and in his eyes she saw the same dazed look he had worn the day Sarah came in the door with the sunlight at her back. It was a fleeting expression, lost in the confusion of getting ready to leave, yet Amanda felt strange, as if something was happening that she could not understand or share. She wrapped her shawl closer around her even though the night was warm.

Ma and Mr. O'Leary and Hettie carried lanterns. The

road was dark under the arching trees but they had plenty of light to see by. They all walked carefully. No one wanted to trip or stub a well-shined shoe. At Three Corners they could see more lights ahead and behind.

"It feels like a party already," Nan said. "I want to run and sing right now."

"You do and you'll drop the cookies," said Mary. "Carry them right side up, for heaven sake, or they'll be mashed to nothing but crumbs."

"Can't you ever think of anything but eating?" Nan was indignant. "Look at this lovely clear night, and the stars and the lanterns, and we're going to a *party* —"

Amanda walked along beside Mr. O'Leary. Her strange cold feeling had gone away and she was contented. Mr. O'Leary *had* noticed her best blue dress and had remarked that it made her eyes look even bluer. Of course, he had made nice Irishy compliments about all of them, but that was just like Mr. O'Leary. He wouldn't want to leave anyone out. She was still the one he chose to walk with, of course, because she knew him best.

The schoolhouse was already half full when they got there, and ablaze with light. Master Pulsifer had driven nails in the beams and lanterns were hanging from overhead and along the walls. The big glass-shaded lamp from Mrs. Perkins's parlor was on his desk. There was one bench set aside for the baskets of refreshments and the rest of the seats were for the audience. The room filled up quickly. Mothers held young children on their laps and everyone squeezed together on the benches to make room for one more. Many of the boys had brought their three-legged milking stools and sat along the walls. Still more couldn't find a seat at all, but stood at the back of the room. No one minded being squashed or standing. Everyone was laughing and talking.

Soon Master Pulsifer stepped up to the desk and rapped with his ruler for attention. Instantly the noisy room was quiet.

"We are very lucky this evening," he said. "Our good neighbors, the Scovilles, have a talented guest visiting them and they have been kind enough to share with us the pleasure of his company. Not only is he a painter of great merit, he is a musician, too, and it is this side of his talent he will display tonight. Ladies and gentlemen, I give you — Mr. Padraic O'Leary!"

There was a great roar of clapping and stamping of boots and then the room quieted down again as Mr. O'Leary rose and began to speak.

"Sure and the last thing I had in mind was a concert display of my feeble talent at music. Can we not make it a free-for-all, with all joinin' in, now? And you callin' out your favorites? Let's begin with a nice jolly song to start us off and get us acquainted. Then you tell me what you want and if the tune's a new one to me, then someone'll hum or sing 'till my fiddle knows it. Ready now? The first song of the evenin' is especially for one of my favorite young ladies. "Froggie Would A-Wooing Go" for Miss Emily Scoville."

Emily was so surprised she almost slipped from Ma's lap. "That's me!" she squealed. Everyone laughed as Mr. O'Leary played a few introductory bars. He began

to sing as he played. For the first two verses the women and children were the only ones who sang, softly and shyly, except for Mr. O'Leary and Master Pulsifer. By the time Froggie took Miss Mousie on his knee, every man and boy was singing, too.

From then on, there was no hanging back for anyone. The requests came so thick and fast that Master Pulsifer had to rap for order, and to call on one person after another to make sure that everyone was recognized. They sang until their throats felt parched, but no one wanted to stop. Old songs, new songs, it didn't matter. William and Henry Moore sang along with the rest, Amanda noticed, and she nudged Julia to make sure she saw them too. Julia giggled, and Nan whispered, "What did I tell you?"

Steuben Purcell had declared that he wouldn't sing, either, but he did. Steuben was a devil in school but he carried a tune well and sang like an angel.

They sang rounds, and the strong voices carried the weaker ones along and made it all sound fine. They sang "Reuben and Rachel," with the men singing against the women, and some laughing so hard they couldn't finish. Mr. Jeremiah Hancock proposed an old song called "John Riley," and when no one else knew it, he sang it all by himself. He was quite carried away with the occasion. Uncle Bolivar had come all the way over from his farm because he was a School Director and wanted to check on what was going on, and even he sang.

Finally Master Pulsifer looked at his big pocket watch and rapped for quiet.

"Friends," he said, "it seems a shame to bring this entertainment to an end, but then it would be just as much of a shame to neglect the refreshments that all you ladies have been kind enough to provide. Shall we rest our throats for awhile — or rather, put them to another use? Ladies, will you serve the treats?"

There was a great cheer then, and scuffling to get in line. The slices of pie and cake and the cookies were passed out, and it was to everyone's credit that only crumbs were left over. Then, stuffed to the gills, as Mrs. Nixon put it, they had one more song to start them on the way home.

"Make it a good one," shouted Mr. Jeremiah Hancock, all dignity forgotten. "I vote for Blue Tail Fly".

So singing "Jimmy crack corn and I don't care," the crowd filed out of the schoolhouse. Some of the older students offered to stay and help Master Pulsifer straighten up, but he shook his head.

"Not tonight. Tomorrow is another day and I'll welcome your help before school in the morning. We'll lock it up just as it is, and let the field mice come in for a party if they like."

Emily had fallen asleep on Ma's shoulder before she was even out of the schoolyard. Teen and Toon stumbled along sleepily in the lantern's glow.

"Do you suppose there will be a mouse party tonight?" Teen asked between yawns.

"Faith, and I believe it," answered Toon, unconsciously imitating Mr. O'Leary's brogue.

"Faith, and I do, too," he added. "A fine grand mouse

party with a wee mousie fiddlin' away the tunes as fast as they can squeak them out. And even dancin', without a doubt, them bein' so small and all, there's plenty of room."

"And then they'll take their tiny lanterns and go home to bed," added Amanda, "just the way we're doing. The mother mouse will tuck the little ones in and they'll all fall asleep singing 'Froggie Would A-Wooing Go'."

7

It couldn't last. Even as she wished on every first star, Amanda knew it couldn't last. Just as certainly as the Indian Summer weather would go, one of these days Mr. O'Leary would go. She tried to push the thought away, but it lay there, heavy as lead. Nothing she could tell herself made any difference. One morning he would pack up his paints and hitch up his horse. And where he had been would be a gaping empty hole in her life.

No one else seemed troubled by any melancholy fore-thoughts. They all enjoyed each day as it slid by, warm and sunny and still with the blue haze in the distance. Sarah and Mr. O'Leary painted and drew all day long, and Ma made pies, and every evening the fiddle sang from twilight until bedtime.

After the first few evenings Mr. O'Leary had insisted that all school work be finished before they began to sing. He played softly while they studied — quiet unobtrusive tunes that did not distract them from their sums and spelling. Ma knitted as they worked. She was making a muffler for Mr. O'Leary to wear around his neck. It was from the wool of Mrs. Nixon's old black sheep, not really jet black but a deep mixy brown black. Ma had carded and spun the wool by hand winter before last. It had been intended for a muffler for Pa, but spring and summer chores had interfered with her knitting, and by the next fall it was too late. Amanda was glad the wool was to be used for Mr. O'Leary. If he had to go away she wanted to be able to think of him wrapped snug and warm in the thick soft scarf.

Now at night she wished on the low-hanging evening star, "If he has to go, then let him come back." She put him into her nightly prayers. "Lord, keep him safe wherever he goes and let him come back, Amen." Each night she raced to finish her school work. Amanda, who had always poked along and was usually the last one done! She hurried to fill her slate and close her copybook and then sit close beside him as he played.

One night they toasted chunks of cheese and bread over the fire and drank hot tea as he told them of his meeting with Amanda and Mr. Aaron.

" 'Twas not much like this," he said, "for the cold rain ran down my collar and I was wet clear through. "If it had been an Irish peat fire, now, I could have gotten it going in jig time, but wet kindlin' was something else again. Not only was I miserable in body, but my spirit was sinking lower and lower. I had no home but an open buggy and no friend but my horse, and him not much for conversation. And I was beginning to doubt myself as an artist, for I'd had precious few portraits to paint, and one of them a prize brood sow. Oh, and I tell you, I was in a bad way, when what should I hear on the muddy road but a jinglin' and a janglin'. Friend or foe, says I to myself, it's company I'm gettin' and grateful for it too with all my heart. The jingle wagon turned in under the trees and the driver looked me over, slow and careful. Faith, how I wanted him to like me! I wanted it so bad I could taste it. He nodded and then from out of a bundle of quilts popped a little girl, and I found I had not one friend but two. Then wasn't it all merry between us, with the fire roaring and drying off me wet coat, and the good hot tea and the cheese and bread toasted on a long stick —"

Amanda remembered it all so clearly. The hours of talking and storytelling by the fire under the shelter of the trees, and Mr. O'Leary's fiddle singing in the darkness. But that had been the summer, and this was autumn and before winter came he would be gone.

One evening instead of playing for them while they studied, he drew. He made a portrait of each one with strokes that seemed quick and careless but caught the likeness sure and clear. He drew Ma in her rocker with her head bent slightly over her knitting and smiling her gentle quiet smile.

Hettie he drew laughing, with her tangle of dark hair pushed back from her brow and her eyes crinkling at someone's joke. All of Hettie was there, — her strong young body and her impatience and stubbornness, and the wonderful sense of humor that was her saving grace.

Sarah was shown drawing, serious, sweet, her long slender fingers holding the pencil and one hand resting against her cheek as she concentrated.

Nan's picture was like her at her prettiest. Sometimes Nan looked frail and peaked and weary, but when she was rested her delicate face had an ethereal look. The fair hair that had been cut short a year ago when she had the fever was now long enough to curl down almost to her shoulders.

Mr. O'Leary drew Mary round and complacent and happy, untroubled by the things that lay outside her ken, fully confident that she could cope with any problems, large or small. He drew Teen and Toon together. They were together in everything and would have been uncomfortable if they were separated by as much as a page in a sketch book. Emily was almost asleep. She looked like a little angel, and yet in the cock of her head Mr. O'Leary had suggested the mischief underneath the angel face.

He had trouble with the picture of Amanda. He made three false starts and was not entirely satisfied when he finally finished.

"It will have to do," he sighed, "and my memory will fill in what my hand could not."

"It seems an excellent likeness," Ma exclaimed. "Her hair, her profile —"

"But how do I tell in one picture that she is sweet and bullheaded, shy and adventuresome, forgiving and nettlesome and that she sings like a bird? Answer me that one and begorra, you'll make me the best artist among the livin' or the dead, God rest their souls. No, it's only part of Amanda, and all the parts are changin' and growin'."

Amanda would have liked her portrait to be the very best, but failing that she was pleased to settle for the worst. It set her apart, anyway.

"I'll keep these with me," he said, closing his sketch book. "They will warm my heart when I'm far away, and at every fireside you'll all be here beside me, just like tonight."

Mary dropped her slate. "You're not going away, Mr. O'Leary?"

"Oh save us, that I am. Did you think, now, that I'd settled in to stay forever. To be sure," and here his blue eyes twinkled, "it's been a visit that's gone on and on. You must have wondered if I ever had on my mind to depart. It's been a grand thing altogether, but a man must get on with his work, especially a man with an open buggy and winter comin' soon."

Teen and Toon scrambled onto his lap and began to cry. "No, no, don't go away. We won't let you go." Nan's eyes filled with tears and even matter-of-fact Mary wiped her nose on her petticoat hem. Ma let her knitting fall into her lap.

"When?" she asked. "We've gotten so accustomed to having you —" and Sarah, stricken, said, "I've only begun to learn to see and to draw. A few more days, surely?"

"You promised you'd take time off from the drawing lessons to go chestnutting with us. You can't go right away!" Hettie added her urging.

"All these good reasons," he smiled. "You make it hard for me. Well then, let's be plannin' it this way. If it's fair tomorrow, as it promises to be, we'll gather the chestnuts. And I have a few chores to attend to — some loose boards on the corncrib and the like. I'll draw up a course of lessons for you to follow, Sarah, my dear. You've come far in a short time and will improve as each day passes if you work at it. And the next day I must be off, though it grieves me more than I can say. Winter will come, and I'm wantin' to be settled in a city with work to do before the bitter winds begin to blow. I've my fortune to make, don't you forget, and fame to chase after, and neither will come knocking on the door here to seek me out."

The next day was fair, as the clear sky the night before had promised it would be. Indian Summer still held, and Wahkonda smoked his pipe in the blue distance. Because it was Mr. OLeary's last day, they all went chestnutting, even Ma. There seemed to be so much to say to him and so little time. He carried Emily perched on his shoulder and chattering away like a bright-eyed squirrel. Teen and Toon pointed out their favorite low apple tree as they went up through the orchard.

"The Maiden Blush tree," they explained. "There's only one of them and it's ours to climb. It used to belong to Hettie and Sarah but now that they're almost grown up they don't need it any more."

"Maiden Blush", he remarked thoughtfully. "Now there's an apple I've not known in the Old Country, and a lovely name, I'm thinking, for a lovely fruit."

"I'm glad Hettie and Sarah are almost grown-up ladies, aren't you?" asked Toon. "Me too," said Teen. "Me too," said Mr. O'Leary fervently. Ma caught his glance and smiled, but what the joke was Amanda couldn't fathom.

The path to the chestnut grove rose steeply after they left the orchard. They could look down the hill and see far across the valley. In the still, honey sweet air sound carried clearly. They could hear the distant cowbells clanging softly and the harsher clank of the bell on Nixon's old ram Ranger.

"This is the last time we'll see this with Mr. O'Leary," Amanda thought. "The last time we will be the people we are today. Next time we will be different and older and nothing will be the same."

Her heart was squeezed up into her throat and she was very much afraid that she would cry. The others seemed so happy and care-free as if his going away was too bad, but not really world-shaking. She couldn't bear to walk along and hear Mary say,

"Remember when I was little and I tripped here and rolled almost down to the house?" Hettie added, "We were afraid you were hurt, and when we got to the bottom you were laughing because you had rolled like a ball all the way down. You were really little then, remember?"

Tomorrow I will be old, Amanda thought. I will feel old inside, old and dried up and dead, and I will still be young. The tears welled up in her eyes and she ran ahead of the others.

There was a little meadow right at the edge of the woodland where the steep path leveled off before it climbed again to the stand of chestnut trees. Amanda came up to the meadow in a rush and saw the gentians through a blur of tears. It was as if a piece of the blue autumn sky had fallen to the grass, misty and shimmering in secret there where no one had been expected to see it. She wished she could keep it all to herself, or share it only with Mr. O'Leary, but here came all the rest, puffing up the hill, earthbound and unfeeling, laughing and joking as if tomorrow were only a day like any other. She wiped her eyes hastily and was able to muster up a watery smile when Mr. O'Leary came up to the top and stopped in delight.

"Faith, and you've found us a hidden treasure, Amanda. Isn't it altogether grand, the sky and the flowers and the faraway blue hills? In all my years I've never seen anything more beautiful. What would you be callin' these, now?"

She had thought that she couldn't speak at all, and yet she heard herself say,

"They're gentians. Fringed gentians."

"Gentians, are they? Heaven, I'd call them, and I wouldn't be far wrong."

Sarah stooped and picked one of the raggedy fringed beauties.

"Here, Mr. O'Leary. Wear it in your buttonhole, and when it fades you can press it to remember us by."

It seemed to Amanda as if his voice shook a little. "I'll not be needin' a flower to help me remember, but I'll keep it all the same." He tucked the little blue flower into his buttonhole and smiled at Sarah. "When I paint

you, Sarah Scoville, 'twill be in a meadow thick with gentians and the autumn sun shinin' on your hair."

Mary had had enough of gentians and remembrances. "Come on, we're not even up to the chestnut trees yet and it's past mid-morning. We want to gather enough nuts to last for a good long time. I can taste them right now. Hurry up!"

It had been a good year for chestnuts. They lay thickly on the ground with their prickly outside burrs split and the shiny brown nuts ready to pop out. It didn't take long to fill the packs they had brought. Even Emily had her little bag of chestnuts.

They roasted them that evening over a good hot fire. There was beginning to be a nip in the air again and Mr. O'Leary remarked,

"I have a feeling I've timed my leavin' not one day too soon. There's a ring around the harvest moon tonight and a chill to the air we haven't felt for a while now. Winter's comin' for fair."

"Then the pipe is almost finished," said Nan.

"What pipe is that, may I be askin'?"

Nan explained about Indian Summer and he listened solemnly.

"Saint Martin's summer, we always called it at home, but sure and the good saint wouldn't mind sharin' the season with the Indians, them being the original owners of the land, and all. In Ireland, it's the Little People who were there first, and they're almost gone, like the Red Men."

"Tell us about the Little People, Mr. O'Leary," Amanda begged. "About leprechauns and crocks of gold and all the rest."

And so he told stories while the chestnuts heated in the iron frying pan. Ma had cut a slash in the top of each one and when it was hot clear through, the brown skin popped and split and the delicious mealy nut was ready to peel and eat. They ate hot chestnuts eagerly at first, and then in moderation, and finally because they could not seem to stop even though they were all full.

"Please play, Mr. O'Leary, or we'll all fall asleep right here on the hearth. I've made a real pig of myself and need to be waked up," Ma said as she peeled just one more chestnut.

He played all his jolliest songs and steered very clear of the sad ones. It was no night to be stirred by the aching sweetness of the old love songs either, or the songs of loss and longing and wandering. He played lively jigs and reels and made his fiddle do tricky things that sounded like horses hooves in "Trotting to the Fair," sounds that made them laugh. It was a gay evening. Everyone pretended there was nothing special about it, that there would be many more evenings of singing and laughing and telling stories by the fire. When it was bedtime he played the lullaby that Emily had come to expect, and then he let the music drift away as always. Ma lighted his lamp and he said as he always did,

"May God keep you safe and send you pleasant dreams."

Amanda stood by the window a long time that night. She wished on her star, and though it was chilly she waited until the glow from the barn was turned out.

"Goodnight, dear Mr. O'Leary," she whispered, so softly that no one else could possibly hear. There was a pale orange ring around the moon and high in the sky a cluster of mare's-tail cloud foretold a change in the weather. She heard a honk in the moonlit night and saw, as clear as day, a v-shaped line of wild geese stretched out, their long necks pointed to the south. Their powerful wings beat the air and they called to one another, joyfully, as if they were glad to be on their way. When the last of them had flown past the mist-ringed moon and had disappeared into the darkness, Amanda shivered and climbed into bed. It would be winter soon. The geese knew it and had left in time.

The next day Ma did not have to sing, "Arise and shine —". The excitement of Mr. O'Leary's leaving had them all up and stirring. Ma was determined that his going away breakfast would be the "stick-to-your-ribs" kind. She had made stacks of griddlecakes and a great pan of bacon and sausage, besides oatmeal with rich yellow cream and fresh brown bread and hot applesauce, and to top it all off, three kinds of pies. Pumpkin and custard and a deep-dish apple pie so oversized she had to bake it in one of the big flat milk pans.

Ma insisted that everyone sit down to eat, excited or not, while she filled the school dinner pails and packed a dinner for Mr. O'Leary, too. She put in enough for several meals, in case he found himself in an inhospitable part of the country. "Although," she said, "it'll have to be a poor miserly door that wouldn't open to your knock."

Mr. O'Leary laughed. "Faith and you've caught the Irish lilt to your speech, ma'am. It's high time I'm leavin' before you all begin to talk like peat boggers and see the Little People behind every stone wall."

Amanda sat at the table because Ma told her to, but the good breakfast stuck in her throat and would not go down. Her throat was pinched together with misery and she could hardly swallow, much less talk and laugh as the others were doing. She thought that no one noticed her unhappiness with all the conversation that swirled around. But very little escaped Ma's keen eyes, and she laid her hand gently on Amanda's shoulder as if to cheer her up.

It was even worse then. It was better to suffer all alone than to have someone else know and sympathize. As soon as breakfast was over she slipped from the bench and escaped to the porch. Let the others tend to the dishes this morning. She couldn't.

It was still not properly sun-up. Later on the sun might shine through the mist and burn it off, but it was too early for that yet. The morning light came through the fog dimly in a pearly glow. The barn was still shrouded in low lying clouds. There was no view over the valley. The fog lay there like piled up cream untouched by the breeze that blew higher up on the mountain. Wahkonda's pipe was finished, the wind had begun to blow, and Indian Summer was over.

The early morning sounds were thick and muffled. Farther down the hill Ranger's bell clanked with a mushy sound. "Over, over," it said. "Over, over." Amanda had seldom felt so miserable. When Pa died, they were all together in their heartbreak, and there was a cold sort of comfort in that. But in this misery she was all alone.

Mr. O'Leary had packed his paints and his few personal belongings the night before. When the door burst open and the rest of the Scoville family poured out, Hettie was carrying his fiddle case and Sarah carried the basket of food, with Mary keeping a close watch so that the overloaded basket did not spill. Ma held Emily, who was still rubbing the sleep out of her eyes. Teen and Toon each clung to a hand, and Nan hung on to one end of Mr. O'Leary's new muffler.

When at last he had loaded everything into the buggy and was reaching for the reins, the laughing faces clouded over.

"Now, now," he said, "we'll say no goodbyes and have no tears, neither yours nor mine, for I'm tellin' you I could spill over and bawl like a baby for the sadness of leavin'. Let's be merry now, for it's been a lovely time altogether and I'd not wish to spoil it. I'll say my Irish prayer for you all and then I'll go off into the fog singin', and when I return, that's how I'll come back." He hesitated a moment, all the joking gone from his voice. "May the road rise with ye," he said, "may the wind be always at your back, and may God hold you in the hollow of his hand." Then he smiled and began to sing one of their favorites,

Then they danced around the happy pair,
And the fiddler played a lilting air—

The buggy wheels began to roll and he started down the hill.

"Wait! Wait!" Teen shouted suddenly. "Wait! I just remembered something I have to find out!"

He had already vanished into the mist and did not hear her. She started to cry. "I've wondered and I've wondered and nobody ever told me, and now I'll never find out! What *is* a little ting air?"

At that they all had to laugh, even Amanda, although a minute before she would have sworn she'd never laugh again.

"Oh dear little goose," said Nan. "That'll be something for Mr. O'Leary to tell you when he comes back."

"But will he really come back, do you think?" asked Teen.

"Of course he will," said Ma. She sounded so sure that no one could doubt her. "Of course he will."

The school day passed in a slow crawl for Amanda. It seemed to go on forever. She knew her lessons well enough and recited passably when Master Pulsifer called on her, but she felt as if her mind was somewhere else. At recess she joined half-heartedly in a game of Fox and Geese, and most of the time she couldn't remember whether she was a Fox or a Goose. She was glad when it was over.

The sun had finally come through the fog. It was not the warm langorous sun of the past few days. The air was nippy and heavier clothing felt good. Amanda drank her afternoon milk by the fire and then decided that, chilly or no chilly, she wanted to be by herself for awhile. The chatter of the other girls was annoying and distracting and she wanted to think. So she took her shawl down from the nail behind the door and went outside again. She looked over toward the big maple but it was almost bare of leaves now, and standing where it did, it offered neither privacy nor shelter from the brisk air. Beside the porch a great clump of yellow chrysanthemums were still blooming their heads off. The sun fell on the house behind them. Hidden behind the flowers, and warmed by the patch of sunlight she could sit unnoticed by anyone who came to the door.

She told herself that she wanted to think, but brood would have been a better word for it. Her thoughts followed no pattern. Mr. O'Leary was gone. She sat there rubbing salt into the wound of her loneliness. No one else cared. She alone would pine away, until finally everyone would be worried about her failing health. Then maybe they would send for Mr. O'Leary. He would leave his pursuit of fame and fortune and hurry back — but no, it would be too late —

She was in the middle of planning this dramatic scene when she heard footsteps coming up the path. If she had so much as raised her head she would have been seen; but she stayed absolutely still. She'd know soon enough who it was.

"Why, Mrs. Nixon. Come right in." She heard Ma's greeting at the door. Mrs. Nixon answered, "Can't stay long. Just thought I'd run up and set a spell, while the weather holds. We'll be housebound soon enough and dying for a chance to be outside in the sun."

"You're right," Ma answered. "Let's sit on the porch. It's warm enough if we bundle up. I'll get some popcorn to shell while we visit."

They always planted a few rows of popping corn, well away from the big cornfield so the pollens wouldn't mix and spoil both kinds. The baskets of popcorn ears were brought inside, and whenever anyone had a spare minute she shelled an ear or two into the big corn crock. Every minute counted on the farm. No one ever sat with idle hands. Amanda felt a stab of guilt. Her hands were idle. But it was too late now. If she jumped up out of the flower bed some explanation would be necessary and she wasn't in any mood for explanations. So she just sat still.

Ma and Mrs. Nixon talked as they shelled the corn by rubbing two ears together. Amanda could hear the click of the dried kernels falling into the crock.

"Well, I see your visitor's gone," said Mrs. Nixon. "Reckon you'll miss him."

"Indeed we will. I dread bedtime tonight. I don't think the little ones have realized that he's really gone away, but when it comes time for the evening singing — oh my."

"And the other problem. Did you settle that?"

"We talked a long time, Mr. O'Leary and I. She's awfully young and so is he. Young and not settled yet. But he's a fine, bright man and a good one. By the time he comes back with his fortune made — or more likely, a little nest-egg saved — if she's willing, I'll give them my blessing."

"How did she take his leaving?"

"Very calmly. She'll miss him, of course. We all will. It's been many months since there's been so much merriment around this house. But she never thought of him as anything other than a friend and a drawing master, thank goodness. No need to have her mooning around with a broken heart, for goodness knows how long it'll be before he's able to marry." There was quiet for a time, broken only by the dry rattle of the corn they were shelling. Then Mrs. Nixon asked,

"And what if someone else comes along in the meantime and she loses her heart to him. What will happen to Mr. O'Leary?"

"We talked about this too. I made him promise he would not bind her by as much as a word or a look. She's far too young. And he was as good as his word. I don't think she suspected a thing. Of course, you know Sarah. She was so enchanted with the drawing and painting that she went around in a complete daze. Anyway, if it's meant to be, it will be. And I have a feeling the young man won't let any grass grow under his feet, now that he has a goal to work for. We'll be seeing him again before long."

The talk then turned to the Tompkins's expected baby, and to Evalina Pettingill's latest flightiness, and to Mrs. Nixon's daughter-in-law, Clara, but Amanda was too numb to listen.

Sarah — and Mr. O'Leary! She remembered now the

dazed way he sometimes had looked at Sarah, as if his wits had left him, and the way his voice had softened when he spoke her name. But she had thought it was because of Sarah's lovely drawings.

Mr. O'Leary and Sarah. When he came back it would be Sarah he would marry, for she could never say no to him, that was certain. Sarah and Mr. O'Leary. Mr. O'Leary and Sarah. He was Amanda's friend and that was all. He had never intended to wait until she had a chance to grow up. Her heart, that she had felt as heavy as a lump of lead inside her, broke then. And every fragment had a sharp jagged edge.

Mrs. Nixon was saying goodbye, and Ma stood on the steps waving as the little old lady went down the hill. Amanda thought she was sitting still as a mouse but some small movement must have betrayed her.

"Amanda Jane!" her mother said. "Were you eavesdropping?"

With that the floodgates burst. All the tears that Amanda had been holding back for days came flowing out. Ma cradled her in her lap and rocked back and forth.

"Baby, baby," she murmured. "Don't cry, lambie. Don't weep so, my precious love."

It was a long time before the sobs subsided into occasional hiccups. Amanda reached blindly for her handkerchief, but could not find her pocket. Ma wiped her eyes for her and blew her nose on the corner of her big soft apron. When Amanda was quiet again Ma began to talk.

"Mr. O'Leary will always think of you as the very dearest of all the little Scoville girls because he met you first. But there's no accounting for hearts, Amanda, and he lost his completely the first minute he saw Sarah. Remember, she's almost a woman grown, and you have years of growing up ahead of you. Wait, and your turn will come. You'll see. Someone as fine and good as Mr. O'Leary will see you and there'll be nobody else in the world for either of you."

"D'do you really th-think so?" she hiccupped. She didn't feel very grown up, sitting like this on Ma's lap and not even able to blow her own nose.

"I know so. And now shall we go in and start supper? It's getting late."

"I'll n-ever be able to eat ag-gain." Yet, as she said it, she felt a pang of hunger in her stomach. Not in her heart, her stomach. This was part of growing up, then, she decided. Getting a broken heart and having it start to heal, and going in to a warm bright house for supper.

8

THAT GRAY Tuesday morning Amanda got up out of the wrong side of bed. On the whole she was a fairly cheerful girl, but some days nothing went right, and almost at once she knew this was going to be one of those days. To begin with, the dark clouds had been gathering for several days and on Monday everyone was predicting the first snow of the year. But instead of snow this morning there was the spit of rain against the window, a particularly cold disagreeable kind of rain. Then, Mary had been worse than usual about her cover grabbing and twice Amanda had awakened, frozen almost stiff, to find Mary firmly entangled in two quilts, with not even a tail left over for Amanda's feet.

Ma was firm about long underwear by November first, so there was that nuisance to struggle with. Amanda's long woolen drawers fit tight to her legs when she put them on fresh Sunday morning. They were still fairly snug on Monday, but by Tuesday the legs had stretched out. They had to be pulled tight and lapped around the ankle tightly with one hand while the other hand quickly pulled up her long black stocking. It called for good planning and fast action or the edge of the drawer went up with the stocking, making an uncomfortable bulge farther up her leg.

She didn't seem to be capable of either planning or action this morning. It didn't help any to see that Mary got her stockings pulled up smoothly on the first try. Amanda gritted her teeth and lapped the miserable drawer leg again. Again it got away from her. She picked up her shoe and threw it at Mary who looked up in surprise as the shoe hit the wall, missing her by a wide margin.

"For heaven sakes, Manda! What's eating you?"

"It's these hateful underdrawers! I'm just not going to wear them, that's all!"

"Ma says we have to —"

"She won't know unless you snitch — which you probably will, you little snake-in-the-grass."

Mary was hurt at this uncalled-for insult. She finished buttoning her shoes and went downstairs, stopping only to say fervently,

"If you're going to be like this all day, Manda, I hope you get what's coming to you!"

Amanda was a little ashamed of herself. Mary didn't snitch often and it wasn't fair to take her bad temper out on the little girl. But her wrath rose up again as she struggled once more with the stubborn drawers. After another failure she snatched them off and threw them under the bed. She hunted hastily for her thin summer underwear. This time the stockings pulled up smoothly and she finished dressing quickly. She raced through her morning chores, keeping well out of Ma's path so her mother's sharp eyes wouldn't notice her suspiciously slim legs.

On the way down the mountain lane she knew she had made a mistake. The cold rain blew under her skirt and shawl and her legs, from her shoe-tops to her knees were soon wet through. She tried to keep her teeth from chattering so Sarah wouldn't notice her treachery. She'd be wild, and she *would* tell. It was Sarah's duty to look after the younger ones and keep them in line, and if they disobeyed she was supposed to report it.

Amanda was glad when Julia and Thomas Perkins joined them at Three Corners. She and Julia hurried on, complaining to each other about the disagreeable rain that had promised to be snow.

There was no playing out in the schoolyard before the bell rang. They all shoved inside to hang up their wet shawls and coats in the cloakroom. Apparently Master Pulsifer was having a bad day, too. The fire was smoking obstinately and little warmth came from the stove. Hennie Hadley held his wet mittens too close to the fire and one of them scorched. The whole room was full of the smell of wet clothing and green kindling wood and scorched wool.

When the lessons began Amanda discovered that in her haste to leave before Ma noticed her lack of warm drawers, she had forgotten her slate pencil. And as luck would have it, Julia had only one. She loyally broke hers in half and handed the longest piece to Amanda. Instead of feeling glad of a friend like Julia, the kindness only made Amanda feel worse by contrast. And so the day went. She stumbled through her lessons and was almost always wrong when Master Pulsifer called on her for an answer.

She had rushed through breakfast, and long before lunch her stomach began to rumble hungrily. If only dinner time would come, she thought. She folded her arms across her stomach and pressed tight to control the noise. Julia leaned over and whispered,

"Don't you feel well, Amanda? You've acted funny all morning."

That was the last straw. "Mind your own business!" Amanda snapped. To Julia! To her best, dearest friend! Julia's eyes filled with tears as she moved as far away as she could on the double seat they shared.

"If that's the way you're going to act," she whispered proudly, "I don't care if I never speak to you again, Amanda Jane Scoville. I don't care if you *throw up!*"

When dinner time came at last, Master Pulsifer looked out the window and announced that the rain had slacked off and would probably stop soon, but that it was still too wet to go outside. Julia took her dinner pail and moved across the aisle to squeeze in with Dolly and Alice — with Alice, of all people! — to eat her lunch, and left Amanda alone in her soggy misery.

By three o'clock she felt as if the horrible day had been

going on forever. She could hardly wait to get home, although something unpleasant would undoubtedly happen there, too. To her surprise, when Master Pulsifer closed his book and said good afternoon to everyone and they had all raced out the door, the afternoon did begin to improve a little. She and Julia walked along together because they always did. Just the same, Julia was noticeably chilly and silent until they paused at the Perkins gate.

"Never let the sun go down on your anger," Ma always said. If she let Julia go in without patching up their quarrel, the sun would go down on anger and it would be harder than ever to make friends tomorrow. Amanda spoke quickly before Julia could open the gate.

"I — I'm sorry I was so hateful, Julia. I don't know what made me act so mean."

Julia's smile was like sudden sunshine. "I'm sorry too, Manda. I don't have any fun when we're not friends."

Amanda was still feeling touchy enough to say, "Well, you were having lots of fun eating your lunch with that Alice!"

"I guess I have a right to eat my lunch where I please, Amanda Scoville. If you didn't want me, I had a right to go where I was welcome. So there!"

"Oh, Julia, here we go again. I don't know what gets into me some days. I want to be friends, honest I do. And I *was* nasty at lunch time."

Julia was a forgiving soul. She smiled again. "We're best friends, Amanda, and you know it. Just the same

I'd better go inside before you bite my head off." She waved and ran up the walk to her house. At the door she turned and called,

"You'd better get to bed early tonight, and watch what side of your bed you get out on tomorrow."

Amanda cheered up once she was on good terms again with Julia. It was a better day already. The early morning rain had stopped and the sky had the leaden look that comes before a snow storm. It was colder, too. Maybe they'd have snow by tomorrow.

Ma thought so, too. When they puffed up to the house Ma checked quickly to see if Nan had wet feet. Nan had grown so much stronger over the summer that she was going back to school again this year instead of studying her lessons at home. But Ma still double-checked to see if she was warm enough and rested enough and eating enough. She had been very sick with the fever and she needed extra care. Amanda took advantage of Ma's concern with Nan to slip upstairs and put on her long woolen underwear. It felt good next to her chilly legs. Surprisingly enough, her clean stockings went on easily over them with no trouble at all.

Ma had warm milk and cookies for them. As they were eating she said,

"I've been watching the sky all afternoon. It looks like snow before morning to me. Do any of you feel equal to going back down to Mrs. Hopkinson's with the carpet rags? Maybe Mrs. Hopkinson can get the carpet done before it gets too cold. You can take the wagon. If we wait until after snowfall it's hard to get the wagon down the mountain road, even if George Warren did fix it up wonderfully. What do you think? I'll do your chores if you're late getting back."

Amanda was the first to volunteer. Now that she was warm and dry and at peace with her little world, she was ready for anything, especially if it involved a trip.

"We really should have a loom of our own," Ma was thinking out loud. "Your Pa was planning to make me one, but first we had to build another room to put it in. We could braid a rug ourselves, but that would take all winter. I want a warm carpet before that wind comes whistling down from the mountain. And we do have a little money this year to pay to have things done."

Hettie and Sarah were willing to go too. Nan would have enjoyed it but Ma shook her head.

"You've been out long enough today, Nannie. There'll be plenty of time for wagon rides when it isn't so raw and cold."

Mary thought it over carefully and decided that she preferred the warmth of the house and would pass up the trip to Mrs. Hopkinson's.

"I don't like Alben Hopkinson, anyway, not one bit. He always pulls my hair and teases so and his jokes about me aren't funny. He calls me Mary Shovel instead of Scoville, and once he yelled, right out in front of everybody,

'Mary Shovel lives in a hovel,

And wherever she goes, she always makes trouble.'

Everybody laughed. Stupid old thing, he can't even make good rhymes."

"Tease him back," suggested Hettie. "I'll help you think of something." But Mary still decided to stay home, so Hettie and Sarah and Amanda bundled up warmly and started out.

Hettie hitched Royal George to the wagon and Sarah and Amanda and Ma carried out the sacks of rolled up carpet strips. They were bulky and clumsy to handle. The inch-wide strips of cloth from worn out woolen clothing and blankets were sewed together and rolled into balls to furnish enough material for a carpet to cover the whole room. They heaved the sacks into the back of the wagon and climbed up to the high seat. Ma clutched her shawl around her and waved.

"Don't loiter," she warned. "Dark is beginning to come early these days, and it'll be getting a lot colder."

They nodded and waved and Hettie started George down the road. The Hopkinson place was not far, a few houses beyond the school, along the valley road. There were four Hopkinson children, all young, including Alben, whom Mary could not stand. Amanda was neutral about Alben, but then, she thought, it's very easy to be neutral about someone if he's teasing someone else. It all depends on whose bull is being gored.

Mrs. Hopkinson was glad to see them. The children were playing out in the yard and they hurried to open the kitchen door for the visitors.

"Maw! Maw!" Alben bawled out, "It's the Scoville girls with a load of carpet rags."

Mrs. Hopkinson got up from her loom. "Well, ask

them in, son, don't stand there gawking. Come in and get warm, girls. It's getting colder out, I do believe. Here, take off your things and stand close to the fire while I finish off this row. Once the little ones come in from outdoors there's so much bedlam I can't do a thing until they're asleep."

"We mustn't interrupt your work, ma'am," Sarah said politely. "Ma wanted us to bring her strips down so you could weave them up whenever you have time."

"You've come at a good time. I have about three feet more on the Perkins stair carpet and then I'll begin on yours. I talked to your ma about it one Sunday after church and I know just how she wants it."

Mrs. Hopkinson's hands and feet moved quickly as she talked. The worn wooden shuttle flew back and forth. She pressed the foot pedals that alternately raised and depressed the warp — the strings that ran up and down the length of the carpet. The shuttle was like a huge wooden needle that threaded its way first over a string and then under, drawing behind it a strip of colored cloth. A beater bar came down to press each strip close to the one before it. It all happened so fast that it was hard for the eye to follow, but Mrs. Hopkinson never made a false move.

After they had seen the process repeated a few times Amanda and Hettie lost interest. But not Sarah. She stood as close as she could to the loom and watched eagerly.

"Want to try it?" Mrs. Hopkinson asked.

Sarah nodded and sat on the bench. She put her feet on the treadles and pressed timidly, pushing the shuttle gingerly through the strings.

"No, not like that. You have to be bold and firm when you're weaving. You have to show the loom who's boss. If you're meek and rabbitty it will take forever and the threads will snarl, and oh, what a mess! See, do it this way — give the shuttle a heave that sends it all the way across, then have your hand ready to catch it and shoot it back again — no, no, change the treadles — see? Now you have it! Try it again."

Sarah's eyes were glowing with excitement. She heaved the shuttle back and forth. Awkwardly at first, and then very quickly she got the hang of it and did a few rows so neat and tight that Mrs. Hopkinson was amazed.

"Well, look at that, will you?" she said to Amanda and Hettie. "I never saw anyone catch on faster. You'll make a good weaver, Sarah, that you will. No reason why you shouldn't. I've heard tell that your grandmother could turn off a length of carpet so fast your eyes'd bug right out. Your ma, too, when she was at home, had a clever hand to her."

"Can you do the fancy weaving with flowers and things?"

"Pattern weaving? Nope. Oh, I could, I suppose, but it takes a kind of patience I don't have. Patience and time. You have to follow the pattern exactly if you want it to come out right, and with the interruptions I have around here — Catherine, either come in or go out and

shut the door! — I just couldn't be bothered. It's mighty pretty, though. Your grandma made a beauty of a coverlet once, Whig Rose, it was called. Just beautiful. Alben, no more cookies!"

It was easy to see what Mrs. Hopkinson meant by interruptions. One of the children was in or out all the time. Little Annie popped in now to say,

"Why don't you big girls come out and play Run Sheep Run with us?"

"That's the kindest favor we could do for Mrs. Hopkinson," Hettie said softly. "Come on, Amanda, let's run the legs off these wild little ones and they'll be so tired they'll fall asleep right after supper. You know how glad Ma is sometimes when Teen and Toon and Emily finally give up and go to sleep."

Hettie and Amanda wrapped up again in their outdoor clothes and went out, but Sarah was too fascinated by the weaving to leave. The four little Hopkinsons went down in steps from Alben, who was eight, to Catherine, to Ella, to Annie, the youngest. There weren't really enough to play a good game of Run Sheep Run so Hettie suggested Tag instead. She counted out to see who would be It.

"Intery, mintery, cuttery, corn,
Apple-seed and apple-thorn.
Wire, briar, limber lock,
Six geese in a flock,
Seven swans by the spring,
O-U-T, you're out again."

Alben was It. Hettie saw to that. Hettie had long ago figured out all the counting rhymes and she knew just which person to start with to make it come out the way she wanted.

Alben started out in a rush to tag Amanda or Hettie, scorning to chase one of the little ones who would be easy marks. Long-legged Hettie dodged and twisted easily. Try as he might he couldn't get anywhere near her. Then he chased Amanda and found her as hard to catch. When Amanda was breathing hard Hettie cut across his path again the way a clever fox diverts the hounds. He was off again after her.

"Chase me, chase me!" screamed Annie, but Alben ignored her. He was puffing and redfaced when Amanda cut in again. She slowed just enough to let him think he could tag her and then darted away. At last he stumbled over a clump of grass and flopped, completely winded, on his belly. Amanda ran to help him up and as she pulled on his arm he panted, "You touched me. Tag, you're It."

"Why you're out of breath, Alben," she said in innocent surprise. "A big boy like you! Did you ever see our little sister Mary run?"

"Never noticed she could run so fast," he muttered.

"Oh, she spares herself around the school. She probably doesn't want to show up you others. Why, if she ever exerted herself — My! Look out, I'm It!"

She chased after Annie and Ella and Catherine. It was hard work to time it so they wouldn't get caught until they had had a good tiring run. Then Catherine was It and she tagged Alben. He went after Hettie, shouting, "Scoville, Shovel, lives in a hovel!"

Hettie slowed long enough to call back, "I'm no good at rhymes, but you'd better not say that to our little sister Mary. She might rhyme Al-ben and pig-pen so fast your ears would whistle." Amanda added, "Did you ever hear the one about Joe Jenks? Everybody laughed for weeks."

That's shaving the truth pretty close, thought Amanda. Mary never made up a rhyme about Joe in her life. But then I never said she did.

"And pull hair! If that little girl ever got mad enough she could probably pull a boy's hair out till he was bald as an egg."

Alben stopped running. "No hair *at all?*" he asked.

"Bald as an egg," Hettie answered cheerfully, as if it were something that Mary might do any day of the week. She came close and let Alben tag her and took off after the girls again. Alben dropped out of the game and leaned against a tree, deep in thought.

It had been growing darker and grayer by the minute, but they were too busy to notice. Suddenly something cold and wet brushed Amanda's cheek.

"Snow!" she shouted. "Hettie, it's snowing, and it's almost dark. We've got to get going." They all hurried inside, red cheeked and breathing hard from all that running in the cold air.

"They'll be asleep early tonight," Amanda whispered to Hettie, who answered, "Don't think I won't, too. I'll likely fall asleep on the way home. Sarah, we've got to go. It's almost dark, and it's starting to snow."

Sarah was standing there with a delighted smile on her face, holding an unwieldy bundle of odd sticks and strings, and a carved picture frame. Mrs. Hopkinson said briskly,

"Now don't thank me, Sarah, my dear. I'll consider it a good trade to exchange an old loom I don't need for one of your lovely flower pictures. Take your time making it. I've had that frame for ages and nothing to put in it, so I'm in no hurry. I do hope that all the parts of that little pattern loom are there. They've been kicking around in the attic since Aunt Phoebe died years ago. Your Ma'll know how it goes together, I don't doubt, and if you get into any difficulty I'll help. Tell your Ma she's next in line for carpet and I'll do my best to get it done before hard cold sets in."

Royal George had been waiting patiently inside the warmth of the barn. He seemed to be glad to be out in the cold air again and stepped along at a good clip. Snow was falling lightly and steadily in the gray dusk. If it kept up the ground would be white by morning.

Sarah was excited by her newly acquired loom. "I've wanted and wanted to learn pattern weaving, and now all of a sudden I've got a table loom of my own. I can hardly believe it. Can't you make George go faster, Het? I can't wait to get home and get it set up. Mrs. Hopkinson gave it to me in exchange for a flower painting to fit this frame. Any flowers I want — I think a mixture would be nice —"

Sarah stopped chattering to dream happily of her loom and her painting. Hettie and Amanda were remembering the thoughtful look on Alben's face when he said goodbye.

"She won't have any more trouble with him," Amanda remarked suddenly out of a long silence.

"Who won't?" Sarah was puzzled, but Hettie understood.

"Mary won't. You can bet young Alben will think twice before he teases Mary again. We persuaded him that she's the fastest runner, sharpest name caller, and hardest hair puller in the whole valley."

"But that's not true. It's fine to protect your sister, but it's wrong to lie, even in a good cause."

"Who lied? We didn't, did we, Amanda? We said *if* she ever got mad enough she'd *probably* pull all his hair out."

"And we just said, 'If Mary ever exerted herself, Oh My!' We didn't say she could run fast, he just thought we did."

"Just the same, that's tampering with the truth, and you know it. But if it makes life easier for Mary, I guess it's justified. Alben is an awful tease and he picks on Mary all the time."

Amanda was silent. She had picked on Mary this very morning for no reason at all except that her underdrawers were lumpy and Mary's weren't. Well, she'd be especially nice to her tonight to make up for it. And she and Hettie had given Alben Hopkinson something to think about.

Royal George jogged along. It was dark now, but the old horse knew the familiar way home, dark or light. The steadily falling snow was beginning to lie on the ground and tree branches now. By morning it would be thick and deep and white and wonderful. Tomorrow would be another day, a better one, Amanda promised herself. A good day from beginning to end.

Ma was as enchanted as Sarah when the odd jumble of sticks was brought in.

"A pattern loom. Oh, Sarah, this is wonderful. Can we get it together properly, do you suppose? It's been a long time since I worked on my mother's loom. I reckon I haven't forgotten everything I knew, though. We'll keep trying until it goes together right. Get washed up for supper now. We've all eaten long ago, but there's plenty of stew to warm your chilly innards."

They ate quickly for they were hungry, and washed the dishes quickly, too. There were lessons to study for tomorrow, and besides they could see that Ma was itching to begin assembling the little loom on one end of the long table. She tucked Emily and Teen and Toon in bed and sang Froggie to them for a few minutes. For once the twins didn't beg for more. Tomorrow they would be up early to play in the snow.

The clock ticked away softly in the quiet room. Ma arranged and rearranged the worn sticks and when she was certain she had it right she untied the little bag of wooden screws that Mrs. Hopkinson had sent. Sarah had a hard time keeping her mind on her schoolwork. She raced through her sums so she could help Ma. Amanda had almost finished her work when she remembered Alben.

"By the way, Mary, I don't think you'll be bothered much by Alben Hopkinson. Hettie and I put a bee in his bonnet."

"What happened? What did you do?"

Hettie grinned at Mary across the table.

"Oh, we just dropped a few words in the right places," she answered airily. "You won't have to worry about him anymore."

Sarah was busy with her figuring and didn't look up. She heard, though, and shook her head as if she disapproved of the methods Hettie and Amanda had used. But the dimples in her cheeks deepened and Amanda felt sure she was trying to hide a smile.

9

THE NEXT DAY was pure delight. The whole world lay rounded and drifted and heaped and piled with snow. There was not a sharp corner to be seen anywhere. The roofs of the outbuildings were curved, every fence post wore a puffy crown. The branches of the fir trees bowed to the ground with the weight of the thick wet snow. The windows that faced toward the mountain were covered where the wind had blown against the panes of glass. The front windows were clear and the immense whiteness outside made everything in the whole room stand out in sharp detail.

Amanda hurried to be the first one outside. She wanted a moment to savor the wonder of the new fallen snow, untouched even by a rabbit's footprints. She stood on the porch, reluctant to make the first mark on the untracked whiteness.

"It's as if no one had ever been here before — as if we were the first people in the world," she said as Mary came out the door. "I hate to step on it and spoil it."

"That's silly," said Mary. "If you don't make the first

step I will, or Hettie or Sarah. You go first because you're taller, and I'll follow in your tracks."

Amanda sighed. The pigs had to be fed, she knew, and the chickens. And by the time the barn chores were done there would be footprints all over the place.

"Listen to the quiet," she said as she and Mary slogged through the drifts. "It's so quiet you can hear it."

"Of all the silly ideas! How can you hear quiet? If there isn't a sound, there isn't anything to hear. Oh dear, I didn't think that drift was so deep. I've got snow down in my shoes."

It *was* quiet. After days of blowing leaves and bare branches rattling and breezes that sighed around the house corners, it was quiet. The little birds that later would peck in the snow for crumbs were still huddled silently in the shelter of the pine woods. There was a deep stillness over everything. In spite of what Mary thought Amanda knew she could hear it.

The stillness was broken when she went into the pigsty, holding her nose against the smell. They kept their pigs clean, but after the clear sweetness of the winter air, even the cleanest pigs were smelly. They were glad to see her, though, with her pan of warm mash and table scraps. They were pleased to have their breakfast.

Hettie and Sarah had decided to shovel a path to the barn and Amanda could hear them laughing and calling as they worked. They'd be glad of breakfast, all of them. Amanda's mouth watered as she thought of it.

Ma believed in a good hearty breakfast, and hearty dinners, too. Nan had the dinner pails filled by the time the other girls had finished the outdoor chores. Ma was cooking breakfast. Hot mush and milk this morning, and dried apple slices stewed to a delectable softness, and thick slices of bread toasted on a long handled fork over the fire.

Ma checked to see that each one was warmly dressed, and that each one had mended mittens and woolen hoods. She sent Nan back to her bedroom for an extra pair of stockings and another flannel petticoat. These she wrapped into a tight bundle and handed to Sarah, saying firmly,

"See that Nan changes into these as soon as she gets to school. Her clothes will be soaked by the time she gets there and I don't want her sitting all morning in damp clothes."

"But Ma —" wailed Nan. "Why? I'll dry off by the fire, just like everyone else, and anyway, where would I change? I can't take off my stockings right in front of everybody, even if my clothes are wet."

"No back-talk, Nan. We're not going to worry through another winter of sickness just because of stubbornness. Change in the privy."

"I'll freeze —"

"You'll freeze if you don't — or you'll stay home and get your behind warmed, young lady. Sarah, see that she minds me."

Amanda knew that Nan was well again if Ma was speaking firmly to her. When she had been so sick and weak for months after her illness everyone had babied and protected her. If she was in line for one of Ma's talking-tos then she was better. Funny how a scolding could be a good sign. Nan sighed again,

"Oh Ma! The privy! It's cold and drafty—," and then gave up after a glance at Ma's determined expression. It was true, the girls' privy in the back of the school yard was not as windproof as the one Pa had made for them behind their own house. He had built their outside toilet well, with two thicknesses of boards so close together that no wind could blow through. But it was cold all the same, unheated of course, even though it was sheltered by a little grove of hemlocks that broke the force of the mountain wind and concealed it neatly from the house. Amanda always dreaded the run to the privy in the early morning and again before bed. Although the big lantern gave off a little warmth as well as light, it was never enough.

"Take the big sled and at least four of you can ride at once and keep dry," Ma said. "The little red one will do for the babies to play on. Nan, tuck your petticoat under and keep your feet as dry as you can, and all the rest of you do it too. I'll mustard plaster you all at the first sniffle."

Amanda hated mustard plasters, wet burning, horrible things — but they did break up a chest cold, or helped, anyway, along with horehound tea and mutton tallow rub. Ugh!

Hettie offered to pull the sled first while the others rode, but it didn't take much pulling. It was more a case of holding the long sled back when it got to going downhill too fast.

"We'll pack this road down after school," Hettie planned, "and we can shoot down in no time."

"It won't be worth the trouble, Het," Sarah said from her place on the back of the sled. "The freeze isn't deep enough. This snow won't last, not more'n a day or so. Even less if the sun comes out."

"We can lay the ground work anyway," Hettie argued. "If we get it packed flat maybe it'll ice over at night and make a good layer underneath. All we have to do is tramp up and down a few times and smack it flat with a shovel and we'll soon have a chute that will skid us all the way to school —"

"Look out!" Amanda was steering, but she didn't see the rock in the road until it was too late. The sled went over and spilled all of them out into the drifts. Nan and Sarah laughed but Mary sputtered,

"If you can't steer any better than that, you'd better let someone else do it. I've got snow down my neck and in my hood and you don't need to laugh, Hettie. If you were watching where you were going instead of making big plans for an ice chute —"

"Oh hush, Mary, it's only snow. No need to make a fuss. Get off and walk if you object to riding."

Mary reconsidered and climbed back on the sled behind Amanda. They turned over twice before they reached Three Corners. The going was easier there. Several cutters had already gone by and Mr. Larkin had been out with his big broad-runnered pung. They walked easily along in the tracks and pulled the sled behind them.

Julia was waiting at her gate. She shouted in time to warn them of a barrage of snowballs from young Thomas. Poor misguided Thomas! He should have waited until they picked up the Moore boys at the next house where he wouldn't be so outnumbered. As it was, he was overpowered by the girls who caught him and rubbed his face in snow until it was red as a beet. He stamped off, vowing to get his friends together and get even.

It would be hard to study today. Everyone was in a holiday mood and Master Pulisfer would have his hands full keeping order.

"There'll be more'n one switching today, or I'll miss my guess," Julia said and Amanda added, "I only hope it isn't us."

They were early, but Master Pulsifer was even earlier. He had a good fire crackling in the iron stove and benches were drawn up around it for drying out wet clothes. There was no one inside, though. Even the teacher was outside where he could oversee the snowball fights and put a stop to them if they got out of control.

"Now's your chance, Nannie. Change right here in front of the fire. No one'll be in until the last minute."

"But I wanted to play —" protested Nan. Sarah was firm. "You can change your clothes here or out in the privy — take your choice."

"But what if some boys come in, or Master Pulsifer?"

"Don't be difficult, Nan," Hettie said. "You're not stripping down to nothing, you know. Just slip off your wet petticoat from under your dress and put this dry one on. I've warmed it all nice and cozy and you can change your stockings before anyone sees. Sarah and I'll stand here and spread out our skirts and no one could see you if they did come in, so stop being a baby!"

Nan gave in and did as she was told. Amanda's petticoat was damp where it had dragged in the snow but hers would dry out fast enough by the fire. She wanted to run outside and play with the rest of the children. She could hear their shouts and screams and squeals. Loyalty to Nan kept her inside and Julia's loyalty to Amanda, while strained, was strong. She stayed in, too.

"We'll build a fort at recess," whispered Amanda," and lick the stuffings out of the boys." Julia looked too fragile to be a good snowballer. With her blue eyes and long yellow hair and gentle manners no one would have guessed that she had a deadly aim with a snowball. More than one big boy had gotten a surprise last winter when Julia had hit him right on the back of the neck.

They wiped away the steam that fogged the window and looked out at the lively landscape. Everything looked brilliant against the white snow. Red faces, red mittens, bright knitted hats and scarfs, red woolen petticoats that showed as the girls ran for shelter behind the tree trunks. Mary and her friends had sleds and were belly-whopping down the slope that ran upwards to the back of the schoolyard where the clearing met the woods. There were at least four hastily thrown up embankments that would be solidified into forts at recess. William and Henry Moore had attempted an igloo but it collapsed on them. They dug themselves out of the heap as Steuben and Bertie pretended to be Eskimo sled dogs and ran around barking.

When Master Pulsifer rang the schoolbell everyone came inside. They brought their boisterous high spirits in with them. There was stamping of boots and slapping of mittens together, and voices were raised above the usual subdued morning hush. Master Pulsifer couldn't do a lot about it. The snow had to be stamped off, didn't it? And then the wet clothes were laid out on the benches close to the fire, with a lot of comments about "pigs who were taking up the warmest places." Besides, Master Pulsifer himself had come in red cheeked and damp from pulling the youngest ones around on a sled. He had to brush the snow off his trousers and coat, too, just like anyone else.

Only during the morning prayer and the Bible reading was the schoolroom entirely quiet. It was hard to concentrate on lessons with all that lovely snow outside. Master Pulsifer struggled to keep order, but it was an uphill job. Not that there was any real naughtiness or backtalk, because he wouldn't stand for that. It was just that everyone's wits had gone a-wandering. The day of the first snowfall was no time to study sums or hard grammar. After recess Master Pulsifer started a spelling bee. Amanda loved this. It was learning, but learning in a nice way. Master Pulsifer was clever. By each missed spelling word on his list, he pencilled the initials of the pupil who had gone down. The second time around he tested them to see if they had learned from their first mistake. It was embarrassing to misspell the same word twice in a row. Amanda was a good speller and so were the rest of the Scoville girls.

"I guess it's because we play so many spelling and word games at home," she said to Julia. "We're always spelling while we do the dishes. It makes the work go faster."

A shadow of sadness came over her. Mr. O'Leary's music had made the work go faster, too, and she missed him. The shadow passed and the day was bright again. There was no sun and the sky was gray, but it seemed bright because of all the white snow.

They all ate their dinners inside at their desks, but after that they were free to play outside again. Sarah decided that Nan could play in the snow provided she changed again into warm, dry clothing.

"No sitting around in a damp petticoat, Missy," she told Nan firmly. "Before the bell rings, we're coming inside to change your clothes while the schoolroom is still empty. I'm going to ask Master Pulsifer to give me five minutes notice."

"Oh, Sarah, don't! I'll die of shame if you say that right out in front of everybody!" Nan wailed.

"Die then." Sarah could not be swayed. "Better to die of shame, all dry and warm, than of pneumonia. Besides, Master Pulsifer knows you were sick. Think of all the extra work you saved him by getting better this year and coming to school. He doesn't have to trudge up the hill to hear your lessons anymore or write out special examinations. He'd be the first one to want you to stay well."

Sarah went to Master Pulsifer and asked him something

in a low voice. He nodded and smiled across the room at Nan.

"See how easy that was?" asked Sarah. "He's going to give us a warning before he rings everyone in for the afternoon. When I call you, you come, there's a good girl."

Amanda was glad that Sarah had worked it out so efficiently. Sarah was a lovely person, she thought. Full of goodness and kindness and strength, with little of that flashing temper and pig-headedness that often made life difficult for Amanda.

Amanda didn't spend much time dwelling on her own life and character. Not with a whole schoolyard of snow waiting just outside the door. She and Julia whipped into their mittens and were out the door the instant Master Pulsifer gave them permission. To their surprise, the school master joined the snowball fight, too. He said it was because the girls outnumbered the boys and he felt it was his duty to even up the battle. But judging from the eager way he packed snowballs, Amanda guessed that it was not duty alone that brought him into the game.

It was a wonderful battle. The girls had the advantage of numbers, but not of skill. Few of the girls could throw with Julia's deadly accuracy but they kept up a steady barrage, with the poorest throwers working to pack the wet snow into ammunition.

"I hit him!" exultated Julia. "I hit him! I got Master Pulsifer!"

"Serves him right for being on the boy's side," said Amanda. "See if you can hit him again."

"I think it's terrible, a schoolmaster throwing snowballs," said Alice Morris primly. "I think it's terribly undignified."

"Well, I don't," retorted Amanda hotly. "I think it shows he really is interested in his students, so there!"

"Well, I think —" began Alice.

"Oh, hush," said Julia rudely. "Don't think, just make snowballs. Hurry, I'm almost out!"

The first snowfall always brought out the general in Julia. She directed the maneuvers of the girls' side and organized daring raids on the opposing forts. Usually Amanda was the leader of the two, and Julia followed. But when it came to a snowball fight Amanda dropped back and let Julia take the lead.

After awhile Master Pulsifer pulled out his big watch. He signalled to Sarah and then went back to the fight.

"That means we've got five minutes to beat them," Julia panted. "Let's storm their fort. Come on, we need more ammunition! Can't you work any faster than — You got him! Good shot, Hettie! Hurry up, slowpokes! Make more snowballs! Move faster!"

"We're moving as fast as we can. And who made you the boss, anyway," Alice grumbled. Yelling like a hoodlum and hollering at everybody to hurry —"

"You're holding us back, we'll miss our chance! Come on, make some more ammunition! Oh dear, it's all over! The bell's ringing."

"I'm glad," said Alice. "You won't dare boss me now."

Somehow — no one saw quite how it happened — Alice fell flat on her face in the deep drift beside the schoolhouse door. She claimed she had been shoved, but if she was, she had no witnesses. Julia smiled sweetly at Amanda, who smiled back just as sweetly. The little mishap put the crowning touch on a very good day.

After school they raced home, eager to get dried off and changed. Ma had hot molasses milk ready for them and freshly baked cookies. The little ones had played hard all day but they were still lively and begging to be pulled on the big sled.

They had managed to persuade Hettie that her idea of a smooth ice-coated chute from the top of the hill down to Three Corners was a mistake.

"It'll be fine going down," said Sarah, "but how would we make it up again? And if we fell, we'd slide all the way down again with nothing to stop us." Hettie agreed to drop her plan and concentrate on sledding, which was more fun anyway. But the trips up and down the hill packed the mushy snow, even without a shovel. That night the temperature dropped sharply and towards morning there was another snowfall, not a deep one but deep enough to cover the ruts their feet and sleds had made. They found the going tricky the next day.

"It's like greased lightning," Amanda said from a snowdrift, where she had been tossed. "You get to going so fast and then smack! the runners hit a rock. I'm going to walk the rest of the way. Give me a hand, somebody. I'm stuck!"

It wasn't easy to walk, either. Their feet slid out from under them at each step. Finally they all floundered downhill in the drifts at either side of the lane. It was slower but considerably surer.

After the Bible reading that morning Master Pulsifer had a short announcement to make.

"Yesterday we overlooked a great many small matters because of the first snowfall. Today's snow is the second and so the newness has worn off. We will expect, therefore, to return to our usual pattern of schoolroom behavior. I'm sure I do not have to remind you that the switch still stands in the corner."

He didn't have to say any more. They would behave or else. So they behaved, with only an occasional restless glance out the windows. After all, there were many snowy days, a whole winter of snowy days ahead of them.

It was that afternoon after school that the excitement began. Amanda was the first to hear the cries for help. The girls had just come home and were changing into the dry clothing that Ma had ready for them.

"What's that?" Amanda asked. "I thought I heard something. Hush, Emily, while I listen." Emily stopped her excited jumping up and down and they all listened.

"Hear that? Someone's calling!"

They raced outside. There was no doubt about it. Someone down the hill was calling.

"Help, help! I can't get up!"

Ma flung a shawl around her shoulders and ran, too. They slipped and skidded down the road almost to the very bottom. There, sitting in a snowdrift, was fat

Cousin Polly Martin, struggling to get to her feet. The snow around her was a witness to the unsuccessful floundering she had done. Poor Cousin Polly. She was round as a butter tub and once off her feet she was helpless and unable to get her balance. She was almost in tears over her predicament. Ma and Sarah and Hettie got her up and out of the snow with some help from Amanda who pushed from behind.

"Oh my —" she gasped. "I never — saw such a road — so steep and under the snow it's slippery — How are you, Sarah and girls — I thought about you and wanted to be sure you were — Help, I'm going down again!"

At the first step forward, she had slipped and was down again, flat on her back like an overturned turtle. Amanda controlled her laughter and tugged. So did all the others. By pulling and shoving, they got Polly up once again. Her face was red from the exertion.

"I declare," she puffed. "I'll never make it to the top! Why you persist in — living on this miserable — mountain when Uncle Bolivar offered you — a place in his big house —"

Amanda slackened her hold on Polly's arm at the very idea of going to live with Uncle Bolivar and Aunt Alberta. It was too horrible to imagine. Hettie and Sarah must have done the same because Cousin Polly started to totter.

"Oh, save me!" she shrieked. "Here I go again! No, don't try to pull me — my arms'll come off, I swear they're frozen stiff!"

Here was a problem. Somehow they had to get Cousin

Polly up the hill to the house so she could get warm and dry. But how could they manage her? She was too bulky to carry, and it was true, they'd pull her arms off if they had to drag her all the way up. It was practical little Mary who suggested,

"Let's pull her up with a rope. If we all helped, we could do it."

"Mary, that's it! Hettie, get a rope from the barn, a strong one, and we'll try it. Now, now, Polly dear, don't be upset, we'll have you out of this in a few minutes. Be patient."

"Easier said than done. It's hard to be patient when you're flat on your back with snow in your drawers."

Amanda covered her face and turned away. Nan's shoulders were shaking. Cousin Polly did look funny but she wouldn't take it kindly if they laughed at her. Hettie was back soon with the rope. They tied it securely around her middle while she protested,

"You'll strangle me, I know it! Oh, why did I ever come here? Oh, mercy, you're cutting me in two —"

"We'll have to snub the rope around a tree," said Hettie, "when we've boosted Cousin Polly to her feet again. And we'll all stay out here in the soft snow where the footing is better. Take it easy, Cousin Polly, one little step at a time."

With Ma pushing from behind and Nan and Mary on either side to steady her, the rest of the girls helped Hettie and Sarah heave on the rope. Slowly but steadily they inched her unwieldy bulk up the hill. Several times she slipped and almost fell but there were enough of them to brace her upright.

The hardest part was to keep from laughing. If Amanda had allowed herself to think of the funny picture they all must make she knew she would be done for. The only thing was to concentrate hard on the work and save the laughing until later. It was slow work and exhausting. They were all panting and red faced by the time they got Polly up to the clearing. She was able to walk much better on level ground.

"Good thing you didn't make a chute out of the road, Hettie," Mary remembered Hettie's plan of the day before. "We'd never have made it."

"Oh, mercy, now that I'm up here, how will I ever get down?"

"We'll manage," Ma soothed her. "Now come inside and get warm and rested. Anyway, you can't think of going home tonight — it's much too late even if you start right now."

"Well, I hadn't rightly planned on going," Cousin Polly admitted. "I thought I'd check on how you all are and stay for a short visit. I told George to expect me back when he sees me. The girls will keep things going at home."

Polly's girls were both grown up, plump as pigeons from all the good cooking that went on at Cousin Polly's house. Of all the relatives they liked Cousin Polly best. A little of her went a long way, it is true, but then they didn't see her too often. She was kind hearted and not as hard to handle as Uncle Bolivar. He was Ma's uncle and had appointed himself head of the whole family to make decisions and hand them down as if they were law. He was so bull-headed that the rest of the relatives lived in awe of him and did whatever he decided was right. Except Ma. Ma defied Uncle Bolivar. He sputtered and blew, but since she was grown and married and widowed, he couldn't force his will on her if she chose not to obey.

So she went right on living on the mountain farm that Pa had cleared, sending her girls to school even though Uncle Bolivar declared that book education past the third reader was a waste for females, and managing in spite of all his dire prophecies about their future.

"My goodness!" Cousin Polly exclaimed suddenly. "I had a bundle with me — my night clothes and something I brought for the children. Where can it be?"

Sarah and Amanda hurried back down the hill and found her bundle in the snowdrift where it had been thrown the first time she lost her balance.

"Nightgown's damp," she said as she unpacked yards and yards of flannel and crocheted lace. Ma hung it close to the fire to dry while the children clustered around to see what Cousin Polly had brought.

"Here's cookies, bust all to pieces, but maybe the crumbs will be tasty. And a bunch of raisins from real sweet raisin grapes, not fox grapes. And a batch of doughnuts, not smashed at all."

Dear kind Cousin Polly. She was funny to look at and had peculiar ways, but her heart was of solid gold. Amanda resolved never to laugh at her again, and then a moment later dissolved into giggles when Cousin Polly got stuck in Ma's rocker and couldn't get out. Amanda couldn't help it. It was so funny. They all laughed and Polly did too.

"This house was made for thin people," she said. "Like as not I'll bust down your bed, Cousin Sarah. I sprung Aunt Alberta's rocker and she's never forgiven me, even though George took it all apart and glued it again. Says I took the creak out of it and it's never been the same comfort for her since."

Cousin Polly laughed until her chins jiggled and that made them laugh all the more. They giggled all evening over their schoolwork. It was hard to concentrate with Polly rocking away, telling all the news of the family as no one else could.

Cousin Polly didn't believe in much education for females either, but she didn't go on about it the way Uncle Bolivar did. It just seemed to her to be a waste of time when girls were going to keep house all their lives, anyway. She never had the time or the inclination to read a book and couldn't see that it made much difference. She was a good wife to George and a good mother to their daughters and when would she have a minute to read?

"Better work on your cooking, children. You'll never catch a man by winning a spelling bee. Have to show him how you can cook. That's how I caught George, on my fourteen egg yellow cake, and take my word for it, that's the way to a man's heart. Book learning won't cut much of a swath compared to a good pie."

Cousin Polly stayed for two days, at night squeezed into Ma's bed with Ma pushed tight against the wall, and in the daytime talking a blue streak. Finally one morning after breakfast she said, " 'Pears like I should leave now while all the young'uns are here to help me down to the valley road. If I wait 'till later, I'll never get down alone. Goodness knows how I'll make it as it is."

"Don't fret for a minute, Cousin Polly," said Sarah. "Hettie and I figured it out last night. We'll sled you down and you'll be all dry and cozy."

"Sled!" Polly was alarmed. "Oh no! If I came coasting down that hill on a sled, I'd slide clear to Waterton before I got stopped. Oh no!"

"We've thought about that. We'll put a rope on the back of the sled and hold you back so you go down gradually. It'll work, never fear."

And it did work. They lashed her securely onto the big sled and then all of them, including Ma and the little girls, hung on to the rope and eased her gently down the hill. Once the sled almost got away from them but they quickly snubbed the rope around a tree and halted its swift descent.

When they reached Three Corners, where their lane met the valley road, they untied Cousin Polly and helped her to her feet. Then they stood and waved goodbye as she started out to trudge the long way home. She would get a lift on the next sleigh that passed, without a doubt, and would stop off for a bite to eat with friends along the way.

"I'll be back when the snow's off the ground," she

called. "Be sure to stay happy and *eat well,* all of you. That's the main thing!"

"Cousin Polly certainly takes her own advice," said Ma. "Maybe there's something to it."

10

"SHH — here she comes!"

Amanda heard Alice whisper and then all the talking stopped. There was an awkward shuffling of feet and no one in the little group of girls could think of anything to say. Finally Ruthie suggested that they all play Red Rover. The girls agreed too quickly and eagerly, and ran to their places.

Amanda did not join them. She walked slowly to the big beech tree at the edge of the schoolyard and leaned against it. The air was cold but the sun had warmed the rough bark and she was sheltered from the wind and the curious stares of the other girls. Ma had warned them that it might be like this and she had thought she wouldn't mind. But she did.

The strangeness had started on Sunday.

The Scovilles didn't attend church every Sunday in the winter. The walk was too long and cold when the weather was bad. But whenever it was possible Ma got them all dressed up and off to church. Last Sunday had been bright and clear, with snow melted in all but a few patches in the fields. Emily and Teen had slight sniffles so Ma decided that all three of the youngest ones should stay at home with Hettie to mind them. Hettie was glad of the chance. She didn't care at all for Mr. Ewing's long-winded wandering sermons and often complained about sitting through them.

"He goes on and on," she said to Ma. "He does all the things Master Pulsifer teaches us not to do. He gets off the subject and hems and haws and rocks back and forth on his heels —"

"Never you mind," Ma always said. "It's not fitting for a young girl to criticize her elders, especially a preacher. Although," Ma admitted honestly, "he's not altogether my dish of tea, either. Sometimes I find my mind is off somewhere else when I'm listening to him. He twists and turns so that he loses me completely."

"I like him," Mary put in unexpectedly. "He does so many funny things that I never get tired of watching him. I can sit there and wonder if he'll fall over on the next rock backward, or try to guess how many times he'll blow his nose or say 'And now to conclude'. As near as I can tell his record is nine times before he really concluded. Once he made it on the first try."

"Mary! That's awful!" Nan was shocked. "He's a preacher. You don't sit and guess things during a sermon. You don't —"

"I do," said Mary. "You can think what you please, but if I didn't count the nose-blowings, I'd wriggle and fidget and that's worse, a whole lot worse."

Nan admitted reluctantly that Mary was probably

right. "I like the Bible the way Ma and Master Pulsifer read it. It sounds good then. Somehow once Mr. Ewing gives out the text I lose interest. But that's no excuse for your behavior," she added sternly.

Ma, with Sarah, Amanda, Nan and Mary, started off to church. They got there just as the last bell was tolling so there was no time for the usual Sunday morning greetings. That would come later when the long sermon was over. The pews were crowded but Amanda found a place next to Julia. They wouldn't talk, of course, not even a whisper, but it was nice to be sitting together, even so. They shared a hymn book, though both of them knew all the hymns so well that they really didn't need the book. Amanda enjoyed the singing and put her whole heart into the familiar melodies. Her pleasure in singing was what tided her over the long dull sermon time. No matter how dusty Mr. Ewing's sermon might be, there would be a hymn or two after it. She folded her hands sedately and tried not to squirm.

As usual, it was not easy to follow Mr. Ewing's line of thinking. He came out strong against Sin, but he was against Sin every Sunday. This particular sermon was even more confused than usual. He seemed to have someone in mind for he leaned over the pulpit and pointed at the congregation while he exhorted them to cast out the sinner from their midst and thus show the wicked ones the error of their ways. Then he pounded on the pulpit and said that those who sheltered and condoned and comforted the wicked were equally sinful and should be cast out also. There was a great deal of rustling and stirring then, as people shifted uneasily and looked at their neighbors. Who was comforting the wicked? Amanda wondered.

Amanda sat directly behind Ma. Ma did not shift or stir but sat up straight with her back stiff as a ramrod. Amanda gave up trying to follow Mr. Ewing's train of thought and admired Ma's lovely black pelisse. It really was handsome and Ma looked so nice in it. There had been enough wool and braid left over to make a stylish little bonnet. There were many in the congregation who were much richer but no one, Amanda thought, looked prettier than Ma. After the service was over, all the families would linger in the churchyard, the men talking about the crops and the winter chores and the ladies discussing their children and their handwork, all the while noticing who was wearing a new bonnet and who was looking well or poorly.

To Amanda's surprise, Ma did not stay for the few minutes of after-church visiting. The very instant the last amen was over, Ma rose and went to the door. She signalled to Amanda as she passed and Amanda fell in behind with the other girls. They were the first ones out. Mr. Ewing had not had time to reach the spot where he always stood to shake hands with each member of his congregation as they went by. Amanda was glad of that. Mr. Ewing had soft white hand, like a lady's, and they were always damp and clammy.

"Ma," said Nan, "aren't we going to wait — ?"

Ma shook her head and kept on walking. Down the steps, across the deserted churchyard and out to the road.

Her face was set and determined looking. She was upset about something, Amanda knew, but what was it? She whispered her question to Sarah, but Sarah was puzzled, too. Ma was deep in thought and made no comment that would solve the puzzle. It was a silent walk home.

By the time they reached the house, Ma was a little more like her usual self. She felt Emily's forehead and rubbed Teen's chest with warmed mutton tallow. She directed the preparations for Sunday dinner, but without her usual sparkle and fun. Ma was worrying about something and only part of her attention was on the activity that went on all around her.

Sarah was counting out the plates and Nan was setting the table when a knock came at the door. Ma hurried to open it and welcomed old Mrs. Nixon.

"Do come in," Ma said. "Sarah, set a place for Mrs. Nixon. We're just about to eat. Please stay."

"Aimed to," said the spry little old lady. "Had it in mind when I set out. Clara made the dumplings for dinner today, and you know I can't abide Clara's dumplings. Wads of dough, they are. Like to fall through the bottom of my stomach, they're so heavy. So I planned I'd come up and set awhile with the Scovilles and finally out of politeness they'd have to ask me to eat."

They all laughed. Mrs. Nixon was welcome in their house at any time, day or night. Indeed, she had spent many long nights there when Pa and Nan were so sick, taking her turn at the bedsides so Ma could snatch an hour or two of restless sleep.

It was a pleasure to share their dinner with Mrs.

Nixon. There was plenty, and that was a pleasure too. Ma had stewed up an old hen, gently simmering it for hours at the back of the fireplace until the meat was tender and tasty. Her dumplings were light and fluffy and the gravy delicious. There was winter cabbage, cold and crisp from the root cellar and made into coleslaw, and a pumpkin pie. The pumpkins would last well into February in the root cellar. They could look forward to many more pies before the last one was gone.

Mrs. Nixon had a hearty appetite for such a little wisp of a body. She enjoyed the dinner and said so. When it was over and the girls were clearing away the plates, she settled herself into the rocker and said determinedly,

"Well now, Sarah Scoville, I've a few things to say."

"I gathered as much," Ma answered. "Girls —"

"No, let 'em stay. There's no place to send 'em where they won't hear, and besides this concerns them, too, or it will once the word gets around. Mr. Ewing's long-winded sermon set the folks talkin' and wonderin' and there are them as agrees with him."

"But I'm not so sure I do," Ma's soft voice was almost sharp. "I'm not sure where my duty lies. I'm thinking and praying for guidance, and I don't need a flock of busybodies to tell me what is right to do."

"Glad to hear you say so." Mrs. Nixon nodded. "Now all you have to do is make up your own mind what is right and do it, and the devil take the hindmost. If your neighbors don't see it quite the way you do — well, let the chips fall where they may. Your girls are all strong-minded enough to bear up under the whispering and the gossiping, as long as they know what you are doin' is the Lord's will." Mrs. Nixon leaned her head against the back of the rocker and watched Ma through half-closed eyes. What was she getting at, Amanda wondered? When Mrs. Nixon looked like that it meant she was trying to draw something out or prove a point.

"That's just it!" Ma burst out. "I'm pretty sure what is right for *me* to do, and that's to help Essie Worthington have her baby when I'm called, regardless of what Mr. Ewing may say about comforting sinners. But then I think about my girls and I can't help worrying. You know what they're in for, Mrs. Nixon. You know how people will take sides and talk, and the children, too. The young can be mighty cruel."

Mrs. Nixon nodded as Ma sat there twisting a fold of apron between her fingers.

"The Worthingtons're trashy. It's not for nothing people speak of them as the Worth-nothings," Mrs. Nixon said. "Their ways aren't our ways, that's certain. I reckon that'd be considered reason for not helping with Essie Worthington's baby."

"But is it enough?" Ma burst out again. "I keep reading and reading my Bible, the verse that says 'Let him who is without sin cast the first stone.' Mrs. Nixon, if I refuse to go because of what the neighbors say, I'll be casting a stone."

Mrs. Nixon rocked without saying anything. Then she said suddenly, "What do the girls think? Sarah, Hettie, what would you want your Ma to decide?"

They all sat quietly, waiting for Sarah to answer. She said, bewildered, "Mrs. Nixon, we don't even know what this is all about. Ma, is this what you were so mad at in church this morning? You haven't told us a thing —"

"I'll tell you, Sarah," the little old woman answered. "Your Ma has a heavy burden and she's trying to carry it all by herself and it's too much of a load. You know the Worthingtons, over t'other side of the valley?" They all nodded solemnly. The Worthingtons were more known about than known. Several of the smaller ones had been sent to school for awhile. They were sickly looking children with sly eyes and uncombed hair and no interest at all in book learning. Master Pulsifer had tried first to tame them with gentleness and then firmness and the one had worked no better than the other. They had stayed for two weeks, disrupting the orderly schoolroom with their rude remarks and fighting during recess. Master Pulsifer had done his best but it was clear that he was as relieved as everyone else when the Worthingtons left. Occasionally some of the older members of the family were seen on the valley road but mostly they kept to themselves. They never came to church and it was rumored that they were Unbelievers. Stories were repeated about the way the family lived but few people knew for a fact if the stories were true.

Mrs. Nixon said, "Essie Worthington's about to have a baby any day now and your ma has to decide if she'll go to help if and when she's called. The preacher thinks it'll be offering aid and comfort to sinners and condoning their evil ways. That's what he was pounding on the pulpit for this mornin', though he didn't come right out and name names."

"But Ma, what has this got to do with us?" Sarah asked. "You said people would talk and be cruel —"

Ma answered wearily, "If they disapprove of what I am going to do, it will rub off on you girls. There'll be talk and some of the mothers won't want you around their children. That's what I'm afraid of. And I truly don't countenance the Worthingtons' way of living — dirty and shiftless and ignorant. That was a good family a few generations back but the stock has run out fast, it appears. But the little baby can't be held responsible for the way the rest of them live. If I've set myself up as a birthing woman I should go, regardless of what the neighbors say."

"Sleep on it and pray on it," advised Mrs. Nixon. "The answer will come and you'll feel it's right. And now, I'll take my shawl and my leave, for dark comes early these winter days and the afternoons are short. Goodbye, my dearies. May your hearts be as light as your dumplings."

So this was what the strangeness was about. Amanda thought about it in the schoolyard as she leaned against the beech tree. Ma had been right when she had predicted difficult days ahead. The neighbors had started to talk even before Ma had made up her mind what to do. They were all determined to make it up for her. They should have known Ma better than that, Amanda reflected. When the answer came to her Ma would go ahead and do what she thought was right and the devil take the hindmost.

The baby basket was packed, ready to go. After the night Mr. Warren came, Ma kept her basket always filled with all the things she would need. There had been many calls since then and the girls had become quite accustomed to the sound of frantic knocking at the door. Often Amanda went along, for there were plenty of things she could do to be helpful. If there were children in the family, Amanda fed them and kept them busy while the serious business of getting a baby born went on in the bedroom. She heated water and warmed the blankets and sometimes cooked up a good nourishing broth or herb tea according to Ma's instructions.

But if Ma did go to help Essie Worthington, would the girls at school say things? And if Amanda went along, what then? Amanda could imagine, since some of them were busy saying things already. She felt terribly lonely at the edge of the schoolyard. She didn't even have Julia, for her best friend had caught Thomas's cold and was home in bed. She was sure Julia would stand by her even if the other girls didn't, but the thought was cold comfort as she watched Alice Morris and the rest playing Red Rover without her.

That evening was a restless one. It was hard to settle down to homework when they were all listening for the sound of footsteps on the porch and a knock at the door. When at last it was bedtime, Ma said,

"Fetch me my Bible, will you, Nannie? It's time for the reading."

The worn book fell open in Ma's hands and she read in her soft voice,

" 'When a man's ways please the Lord, he maketh even his enemies to be at peace with him.' Why, it's like a sign!" Instead of finishing the chapter as she usually did, she began to turn the pages, reading aloud here and there as she came to a verse that had special meaning for her. The children sat quietly, listening. " 'Be of good courage and He shall strengthen your heart.' 'Whatsoever thy hand findeth to do, do it with thy might —' " She closed her Bible and sat for a long time, thinking. Then she said,

"My mind's made up. If the Worthingtons call, I'll go. It's surely the Lord's work and if I am able to please the Lord in even a small way, my neighbors will not be my enemies."

The call from the Worthingtons came that night. It was getting on towards morning. The sky was beginning to lighten when Amanda heard the knock at the door. She was out of bed and into her clothes almost instantly. Sarah was up, too, and helped her with her back buttons. Hettie, with a shawl wrapped around her shoulders, hurried down the stairs to take something from the oven next to the fireplace. "Meat pastries," she explained to Ma. "I put them in to warm last night, just in case. You'll need something hot before you start out. Goodness knows when you'll have breakfast."

The young man standing by the door said, "I've brung the buckboard so's you'll not have to walk. We can go right fast. She's took bad, Essie is."

"How bad?" Ma asked tersely as she wrapped a warm

muffler around her neck. Sarah stood by with two heavy shawls and warmed mittens.

"Purty bad, I guess. We hadn't figured to get anybody in. Essie said nobody'd come. But something's gone wrong and Grammaw got worried. Gram's down sick with the rheumatiz and can't do much, and she started hollerin' for us to get help, so I came. The kids are screamin' and runnin' around and that don't make Essie feel no better, nor Gram don't either, poundin' on the floor with her cane."

Amanda was dressed in her outside clothes and ready before Ma was. Ma still hadn't said she was to go along, but then neither had she said no. The basket was ready and Ma picked it up and started for the door. Amanda followed close behind her.

"The young'un comin' too?" the man asked. Ma hesitated and frowned.

"Whatsoever thy hand findeth to do—" Amanda quoted. "I'll be able to help you do it with all your might."

"Well, come on, then," the man said abruptly. "Don't stand here backin' and fillin' and wastin' time." He opened the door and went out without bothering to hold it for Ma.

"She'll be a help," said Sarah softly. "And company on the ride, too. You won't get much polite conversation out of *that* one." Sarah looked toward the porch where the man was standing impatiently. "Come on," he said again. Ma nodded to Amanda and they went out together. The man — Amanda supposed he was a Worthington, but was he a son or uncle or father? — made no move to carry Ma's basket or to light her path with his lantern. He said briefly, "Tied the horse at the bottom of the hill," and then plunged on ahead with long strides down the steep road. Ma and Amanda stumbled along after him. The sky was growing light but under the trees it was still dark as night.

"I'm glad the snow's melted off," Ma said once. "We'd have a time getting down here in the dark if it was snowy or icy."

The Worthington man was waiting for them at the foot of the hill. He was already on the high seat of the wagon. He jerked his thumb to indicate that they were to climb in the back. Ma hesitated and he said, "There's hay back there, and a blanket iffen you're cold." He did not offer them a place on the seat so they had no choice but to scramble in the wagon as best they could. He was in a hurry. As soon as they had climbed over the tailgate he slapped the reins and clucked to the horse.

The rickety wagon jerked and jolted over the frozen ruts. Ma and Amanda were tossed unceremoniously in a heap on the wagon bed. There was a blanket, it was true, but it did not feel or smell inviting. "Heaven knows — what — he's been hauling — in — this wagon," Ma whispered. "Better — we don't — know —" Amanda answered. "We wouldn't — be able to sit — down at all like as not —"

"We — certainly couldn't — stand!" They were rocking from side to side and had to cling together to keep from sliding around. The horse, tired of waiting in the cold, seemed glad to be heading home and moved along at a fast, if uneven, speed. Ma finally pulled the gritty blanket over their legs and wrapped her outside shawl around them both as they huddled together for warmth. It would be a pleasant winter day later on when the sun was up, but now, in the very early morning, the cold was raw and penetrating. Amanda was warmly dressed but the cold air crept inside everything. And on top of that she remembered that she hadn't had any breakfast. "I'm hungry. How long do you suppose it will take to get there?"

"It's quite a ride," Ma answered. "Where's the food that Hettie packed?" She felt around in her big basket and found a warm bundle. Hettie had wrapped a hot brick and the two meat turnovers in a piece of flannel, and the pies were as hot as if they had just come from the oven. Ma took them out and put the brick under the blanket by their feet. "We'll keep our feet and our hands warm at least. I'd feel better if I could wash before I eat, but we've no choice."

They were speaking in low voices, but even if they were not, the driver couldn't have heard them over the sound of the creaking wagon. The left front wheel squeaked at every turn. It was annoying at first but soon the irritating sound blended in with all the other squeaks and rattles and they didn't notice it.

"Quick, eat your pie before the sun comes up and he

sees us. We've only two, and I wouldn't want to eat in front of the man without offering him any."

Amanda giggled.

"He'd probably take it all, and no thanks either." She bit into the luscious warm turnover. It was made of finely chopped cooked beef and onions with just enough gravy to moisten it. Ma did make the best meat pies, Amanda thought, as some of the juice ran down her chin. Ma was having trouble, too.

"We'll be a mess by the time we get home. We'll have to sponge our clothes and air them for days to get the horse blanket smell out of them. Here's my hanky. Mop up what you can and don't worry."

They ate their pies and then joggled along in silence. The uncomfortable ride seemed endless, all the way across the valley to the other side. They passed the Warren's neat little house, still wrapped in misty shadows.

"The Worthington house won't be like that," Amanda thought. "Not orderly and clean at all, I'll bet. Not judging from the looks of the children and the wagon, anyway."

She was right. The Worthington house was far from neat and clean, but how far she never could have imagined.

11

THE WAGON creaked into a rutted lane and stopped a short way back from the valley road.

"Here we are," the driver said. They pushed back the blanket and got to their feet. It was hard to get used to standing when they had been lurching unsteadily for such a long time. It was almost full daylight now. They could see the Worthington place clearly and what they saw was not in the least inviting. The house was poor and plain and uncared for. The porch steps leaned crazily and the yard was littered with trash. On the clothesline in the back yard there was a motley row of clothes. They flapped in the cold morning air, ragged and not too clean and frozen stiff. They looked as if they had been hung out absent-mindedly some time ago and then forgotten. A thin dog yapped at the wagon wheel and the driver pushed him away with his heavy boot.

"Well, don't stand there," he said. "Light and come in. There's no time for gawkin'." He made no move to help Ma down so she held on to the tailgate of the wagon and jumped down unaided. Amanda handed her the basket and followed close at her heels as she picked her way through the untidy yard.

The man went ahead, muttering, "Watch that step, it's broke." He pushed open the door and went in ahead of them, shouting, "She's here, now shut up that noise!" He motioned to a steep stairway along the wall and said, "Up there."

Ma hesitated. "We'll need to wash. We can't go into a sickroom like this."

"Later," the man insisted. "Essie's took bad, I told you. Go on up." There seemed to be nothing else to do so Ma started up the stairs. Amanda went too. She had a quick glance at a room full of hostile, curious faces, none of them clean. There were two other thin yapping dogs and several thin yapping children. There was a bent old woman who pounded a huge gnarled walking stick on the floor when she wanted attention. There was noise and confusion, and the man's shout for quiet had had no effect at all.

The stairway led to a loft-like second floor, roughly partitioned off into rooms. Across the open doorway of one a tattered quilt had been hung. From this doorway came the sound of a moan. Ma pushed aside the quilt and they went in.

A young woman lay on the rumpled bed that was the only piece of furniture in the room. She opened her eyes and said weakly,

"You came. They all said you wouldn't, but you did!"

Tears started to flow down her cheeks. Ma handed Amanda the basket and hurried to the bedside.

"Of course we came," she said soothingly. "I brought one of my girls to help. Now you just lie there and rest and stop worrying. Amanda and I will do our best to make you comfortable and get this baby born."

The woman stiffened suddenly and groaned. Ma took her hand and held it tight. In a few seconds the pain had passed. Ma didn't pull her hand away but counted softly until the next pain came. Then she said to Amanda, "I'll need a kettle of hot water and a basin. I have a clean wash cloth. I'll stay right here and hold Essie's hand — there's nothing else we can do for her right now. Take off your shawl and sweaters. We'll be here for awhile from the look of things."

Amanda looked around for a place to set the basket. There was no bureau or chair in the room so she had to put it on the floor. There were nails driven in the wall and a limp dress hung on one of them. Apparently this was the place to put your clothes. Ma took off her outside clothing and hung them on a nail so Amanda did too. Ma unbuttoned the cuffs of her dress and rolled up her sleeves.

"Soon as I wash I'll put on my clean apron. Tell them to hurry with the water, please."

Essie moaned again and Ma turned back to the bedside. Amanda went out through the quilt-hung doorway and down the steps. The Worthingtons were eating breakfast, an unappetizing meal that was flung carelessly on the table. Everyone looked up as she came down the steps but no one said anything to her, nor did they stop the wrangling that was going on. She cleared her throat and said timidly,

"My mother would like a kettle of hot water, if you please." One of the younger children, one of those who had come to school for a short while, snickered. The tall uncouth young man who had driven the wagon motioned in the direction of the fireplace where a kettle was hanging. "And a basin, too," Amanda added.

"We got a basin, Grammaw?" he asked. He made no move to find it, if they did. He went on eating while the bent-over little old woman thought.

"We had a basin onc't," she said. "You young'uns use it for chicken feed? Thought that was what happened to it. Well, don't jest set there stuffin' your faces. Get the girl a basin. Jump, you hear me?" She raised her voice and banged on the floor with her walking stick. Startled, Amanda jumped, and so did a stringy looking little girl who appeared to be about twelve.

"Don't holler, Grammaw," she begged. "You'll upset Essie. I'll find you a basin somewheres," she said to Amanda. There was a cupboard in the room and after a little searching the girl found a good-sized vegetable bowl.

"This do?" she asked. Amanda nodded. "Take it then, and I'll carry up the kettle. Watch out for Tiger. He's mean when he's hungry." She shoved one of the dogs aside, and using a dirty cloth as a pot holder, picked up the steaming kettle. "It's about empty. I'll put on some more when this is used. Come on up."

She led the way up the stairs and into the bedroom, and

then stood watching curiously as Ma poured the water into the bowl. Ma had put a piece of her precious lilac soap into her basket as well as a cake of the homemade kind. She had guessed evidently that soap would be hard to come by at the Worthington house. She washed her hands well and dried them, and then said, "Will you empty this, child? I'd like to wash Essie's face and hands, too. It'll make her feel better."

The girl took the bowl and hurried to the window. It was stuck, but it came open after a little struggle. She threw the water out the window with never a glance toward the ground. She must have soaked one of the chickens that wandered through the yard, for there was a wild squawking and flapping below. The girl shrugged.

"First time they got hit by anything so sweet smellin'. That soap of yours, it smells like flowers. Grammaw's soap smells like old bacon fryings. How you get it so nice?"

"It's store soap," Amanda said proudly. "Ma bought two cakes last fall."

Ma had put more water in the bowl and was gently washing Essie's weary face. "You can use the lilac soap, too," Ma said, "as soon as I finish with Essie."

The girl was suddenly shy. "I got to fill the kettle," she stammered, and grabbing the black iron pot, she fled from the room. But she was back again almost immediately, her shyness overcome by the fragrance of the soap. Amanda could tell by the awkward way she held the wash-cloth that scrubbing was not something she did often.

"Feels good," she remarked dreamily. "I bet you do this everyday, don't you?"

"Well, we only get to use the lilac soap for very special, but Ma makes us wash every day, with a whole bath on Saturday."

"I never get to take a bath. There's always a crowd comin' in or out of the kitchen, but summers I get wet all over, sometimes, in the creek. Someday," she added fiercely, "me and Essie are goin' to have a *tub,* even, and soap and a place to wash in." Then she became shy again and said, "I got to do chores now. Grammaw's all tied up with rheumatiz and her bones ache her, so I do the house chores. Them little ones, all they do is mess things up. They aren't no help at all, hardly."

Ma was tying on her big clean apron. "I'd appreciate a chair or a stool — what did you say your name is, child?"

"I never did say, but it's Rosaline."

"That's a nice name. This is Amanda." Amanda nodded and said, "Hello, Rosaline." The girl's thin shoulders drooped. "I got to tell it true. My name's Agnes and they all call me Ag. But *someday* I'll make everybody call me Rosaline!"

"No reason why you shouldn't," Ma said. "It's a pretty name and you could be a very pretty girl. Agnes is a good name, too. Names don't matter as much as what you are." She smiled at the two girls. "I don't need you right now, Amanda. I'm sure there's something you can do to help Agnes."

Amanda wasn't sure she liked the idea, but Ma's voice was firm so she followed Agnes out of the room.

"I'll take a stool up to your maw. We're a mite short on chairs right now," Agnes said with a kind of pathetic dignity. Short of more than chairs, I'd guess, Amanda thought, but of course she didn't say it aloud. She stood in the downstairs room, empty now of all Worthingtons except the little old grandmother dozing by the fire. There certainly was a lot to do. The whole room was in disorder. It would take hours to scrub and straighten it and more hours to repair the broken chairs and the sagging cupboard door. I've chores enough to do at home, Amanda thought rebelliously. I don't want to do the Worthington's chores, too, not when they won't lift a finger to help themselves — living like animals!

Agnes came downstairs again, looking pale and worried.

"Essie's in bad shape," she whispered. "She's groaning and lashing around. Yore maw's got her hands full but she says she won't need anything for awhile, 'cepting' water." There was a moan from the bedroom and Agnes clasped her hands together desperately.

"I can't bear it if anything happens to Essie," she said. "I know she's not what you'd call a good girl, and the preacher came right out and said she's a black-hearted sinner. But she's sweet and kind and she likes pretty things. That's what started all her trouble, I reckon, she just wanted things nice, and she believed that man when he said he was going to marry her and take her away. Then he disappeared." Agnes' eyes filled with tears.

"She's all I got. There's nobody else who cares whether I live or die."

Amanda felt sorry for this girl who had so little. In comparison, their house on the mountain seemed almost luxurious, clean and neat and pretty, and full of love. She was surprised to hear herself saying,

"You've got me now. I care if you live or die, and Ma does, too. And God cares all the time even when you don't know it."

Agnes shook her head. "We aren't church goin' folks. You know that. God ain't interested in people like us, only in the good ones."

Ma would know the Bible verses that would comfort poor Agnes, but Amanda couldn't think of the right ones to say.

"You're wrong, Agnes. I'm sure of it. God is interested in sparrows, even, and He's interested in you and Essie, too —"

Another moan from upstairs interrupted them, and again Agnes shivered.

"Look," Amanda said. "Ma's a good birthing woman and she'll do whatever has to be done. Just have faith and don't worry and things'll work out." She recalled the long hard days of Pa's illness. "Ma says work is a good thing when there's trouble in the house. Let's keep busy and the time will pass quicker than if we're waiting and fretting. Come on, let's scrub."

There was a teakettle hanging in the fireplace, but that was for Ma's use. Amanda found a battered bucket.

"Where's the water and some scrub rags and a broom?"

Agnes was fired by Amanda's energetic example. "I'll get the things. No, let the little ones fetch the water. Do 'em good to have some work to do." She took the bucket and marched determinedly out of the porch. The younger children were whooping and running around the house.

"You, Mike," Agnes shouted. "Com'ere, fast!" Mike was surprised to find the bucket thrust into his hand. "Bring us water, and the rest of you find something to carry water in. Move fast, now!"

"I don't know who you are to order us around," Mike grumbled. Agnes's eyes flashed. "I'll tell you who I am! I'm Agnes Worthington and I'm about to clean house and you'll mind me or I'll take a broom to you! Quick, get the water!"

The children were awed at Agnes's display of anger. They hurried to find another bucket and a bent tin basin. Once inside again, Agnes's shoulders drooped discouragedly as she looked around the room.

"I don't know as we can do it," she said. "It's so messy and all."

Amanda felt discouraged too, but she had got this thing started and she didn't see how she could back out now. A moan from above set her in action again. "We can do *something,* anyway. I'll sweep and you move the furniture out of my way."

"Most of it is broke," her new friend remarked.

"Pile it up to one side and maybe your father will fix it."

"Not likely. Them chairs have been broke ever since the beginning of time. They get more and more rickety and finally one of the little ones busts them altogether."

Mike appeared at the door with a pail of water. "It's cold," he complained. "My hands like to froze to the handle." Agnes was unsympathetic. "You'll warm up. Dump the water in the big kettle and bring more."

"What you doin', anyway? What's goin' on here?"

"Hush and get movin'," Agnes commanded, "or I'll give you one where it counts."

Bewildered, Mike picked up the empty bucket and went back to the well. Agnes moved the stools and table back against the wall and Amanda set to work with the worn broom. It had been a long time since the floor had been really cleaned.

"Just sweep the dirt out the door," Agnes advised. "No sense in trying to pick it up." Amanda knew that Ma didn't clean that way, but then, she reasoned, a little more trash in the yard wouldn't even be noticed. They worked quietly so that Grammaw Worthington wouldn't awaken.

"She's got rheumatiz bad in all her joints and she can't hear too good, neither. That's why she hollers so. She's got a mean tongue in her head because she's so miserable most of the time. I don't know what she'll say to all this cleanin'."

"We'll work around her," Amanda whispered. "Maybe she won't wake up until we've finished."

"I'll do the floor. No sense in you spoilin' your nice dress. You want to wash dishes?"

The pile of greasy dishes was not particularly appealing but it was at least a more pleasant job than scrubbing the splintery floor. There was plenty of hot water now but the Worthington soap was so poor she couldn't work up any soapsuds. She tiptoed upstairs to ask Ma for the cake of their good homemade soap. Essie had drifted off into a troubled sleep so she took the soap and tiptoed out again. Agnes asked, "How is she?" and Amanda was glad to be able to say that Essie was resting. The girl's tense face relaxed and she smiled as she went back to her vigorous scrubbing.

One thing about chores at the Worthington house, Amanda reflected, they went on and on. When the breakfast dishes were washed and scalded and dried there was no clean place to put them. The cupboard was dusty and needed a thorough cleaning. Amanda scrubbed the big table top and stacked the clean dishes there. She was starting to empty the cupboard shelves when Grammaw Worthington woke from her nap.

"What's this? What you doin', girl?"

Agnes answered soothingly, "Now, it's all right, Grammaw. This here's Miz Scoville's girl, Amanda, and she's helpin' us get cleaned up. This place is goin' to shine afore me and Amanda're through. Lift up your feet onto this stool so's I can scrub around you."

The old woman sniffed scornfully. " 'Bout time we got this place straightened out. With Essie down, things have got worse 'n worse. How is Essie? Miz Scoville say?"

"She's very tired. She's sleeping." Amanda wished Grammaw would lower her voice.

"Why's she sleepin' in the middle of a birthin'? Never knew of any birthin' to take so long. Somethin's wrong. If I could get up them steps, I'd help. You sure everything's all right?"

Amanda answered truthfully, "I don't know. Ma is capable and she'll do whatever is to be done."

The old woman nodded. "I guess Essie'll be pleased to see this room fixed up a little. She likes things nice, and all the work kept a-frettin' and a-naggin' at her —"

The warmth of the fire soon made Grammaw Worthington sleepy again. Agnes had ordered the little ones to bring in more wood and she had a good blaze crackling to dry out the damp floor.

Amanda had washed the dishes from the cupboard. Agnes looked critically at the glass doors and said, "That glass is all grubbed up with greasy finger marks. What do we use to make it shine?"

"Ma uses vinegar," Amanda said. So after smelling several jugs, Agnes found some vinegar and set to work polishing the glass.

"Stinks," she said, wrinkling her nose. "Smells the whole place up."

"Put some pine boughs on the fire. That'll make a good clean smell in the air." Mike was called in again and went with the other complaining youngsters to bring back some evergreen branches from the woodlot.

Agnes apologized for their lack of manners. "We ain't none of us much on manners. My Maw use to try to teach us sometimes, but she up and died four years ago and since then Essie's the only one who notices much what we do. Oh mercy, Essie's groaning again! She sounds terrible!"

Ma appeared at the top of the stairs and motioned to Agnes. She spoke in a low voice, urgently.

"Tell one of the men to go for Mrs. Nixon," she said. "Tell them to hurry." Agnes grabbed her shawl from a nail behind the door and ran out to the barn calling for her father and her brother Eph.

"Oh Ma," Amanda begged. "Don't let anything happen to Essie. Agnes'd die, too, I know she would."

"I'm doing my best, Amanda. I'm doing all I know. Only the Lord can say what will happen to Essie. I keep thinking there must be something more I can do if I had more experience. That's why I want Mrs. Nixon." A moan came from the room above and Ma hurried back upstairs.

When Agnes came back from the barn she was white faced and tense. "Pa's gone," she said. "He threw a saddle on the horse and went as fast as he could. Amanda, what'll I do? What'll I ever do?" Tears started to roll down her cheeks. Amanda seized her trembling hands and held tight. "We can pray. We'll pray as hard as we can."

"I don't even know no prayers, except 'Now I Lay Me' —."

"We'll say 'The Lord is my shepherd'. Say it after me, Agnes, and keep working."

There was no sound in the house except for the fire snapping on the hearth, Grammaw's occasional snores, Essie's pitiful cries from upstairs, and Amanda and Agnes saying the beautiful Psalm. They polished the glass of the cupboard over and over until it sparkled in the firelight. Finally the comforting words had their effect on Agnes. She lost her gray, fearful look and some pink came back into her thin cheeks.

"We've most rubbed this glass clear through. You keep sayin' it, Amanda, and I'll put the dishes away." So Amanda repeated once more, "The Lord is my shepherd, I shall not want," and Agnes put the clean dishes back in the cupboard with the energy born of desperation.

"I'm putting them in nice, the way Essie likes things done. I'll stand the big platter here and put a bowl here so the chipped place won't show —."

Her brother Eph appeared at the door and she turned on him. "Clean your boots," she ordered. "I'll not have this clean floor tracked up. And while you've got your outside clothes on, get all these busted chairs outta here and don't bring 'em back till they're mended. Essie gets sick and tired of having the furniture all broke up." Eph was startled at her vehemence, but he obeyed. There were five chairs with broken rungs or weak backs. Agnes watched while he carried them out to the barn. "Things are goin' to be different around here. By the time Essie is downstairs again we're goin' to have it nice for her and her little baby. What can we do now?"

Amanda saw that the four young Worthingtons were standing on the porch with their noses pressed against the window. "We'll have to get something fixed to eat. Everybody's going to be hungry soon."

"I hate to get them nice clean dishes dirtied. But I

guess if I'm goin' to teach the little ones manners they got to have plates to eat off of. What shall we have? There's potatoes and onions and side-meat. Doesn't seem very fancy."

"It doesn't have to be fancy if we fix it nice," Amanda assured her. "Come on, show me where you keep your things."

The thought of dinner reminded Amanda that she was ravenously hungry. It had been a long time since she and Ma had eaten the meat pies in the frosty dawn. At home a plain meal like hash would be made more interesting with pickles and relishes and applesauce. The Worthingtons had nothing like this on hand. But there was plenty of milk and some heavy bread.

"Grammaw has to have her bread sopped up in milk. No teeth, you know, and chewin's a problem. All she eats is bread and milk."

"Let's make her a good milk soup. That'll be a change. Ma cooks potatoes and onions and mashes them up fine with lots of butter and —"

"There's not a mite of butter. I didn't get around to churning yesterday. The milk's still settin' in the pantry."

"Well, it's too late to churn for dinner, but we'll get it done for supper. Let's skim us off some cream and I'll shake it in a jar until butter comes."

Agnes had never heard of this way to get a small amount of butter. After some searching she found a covered jar. Amanda rinsed it out — everything in the Worthington house was dusty — and after they had skimmed some of the cream that had risen to the top of the milk can, she put it into the jar. Then, while she shook the jar vigorously, she had Agnes scald the wooden churn and butter bowl.

"If it's not washed clean and scalded every time after you use it, your butter won't taste nice and sweet and fresh."

Amanda was not considered a particularly good housekeeper, for she was apt to be careless, but she did know from Ma how things *should* be done. So she did her best to help Agnes, who seemed to be struggling against almost insurmountable difficulties.

Finally dinner was ready. Agnes went to the door to call Eph and the younger children. She carried a basin of warm water and a towel and inspected each face and pair of hands before she let the children in the house. Mike complained that "his skin would be plain wore out with all that washin' " but Agnes was firm. Even Eph did not argue with her.

Mr. Worthington had not yet come back with Mrs. Nixon but they decided not to wait for him. It was a quiet meal. The children were subdued by the neatly set table and by Agnes's whispered commands to sit up straight, keep their elbows off the table, eat with a fork, don't spill the milk. They sensed, too, the seriousness of Essie's condition if their father had had to go for more help. Eph looked wonderingly at his little sister and made an attempt to improve his table manners. Grammaw slurped her soup noisily, but she was old and crippled and Agnes made no attempt to change her ways. Grammaw enjoyed her meal and passed her bowl back three times to be filled.

"You make that again, Ag," she ordered as she wiped her chin with the back of her hand. "Good food like that gives me back my strength. It's better'n that baby pap I been eatin'."

"Glad you got your strength, Grammaw, because now you're goin' to set in your rocker and tell stories to the little ones whilst Amanda and me clean up."

"What's this?" Grammaw shrieked. "What's got into you, girl? I don't recollect no stories!"

"Then you can make some up," Agnes said firmly. "I read in a book onc't that the Grammaw set and told stories afore the fire and the young'uns listened. So you can start tellin' and they'll listen and I don't want no fightin' or shovin' either."

Grammaw had no more than cleared her throat to begin when they heard the sound of horses' hooves and buggy wheels in the yard. They all raced to the window to see Mr. Worthington jump from his horse and grasp the reins of Mrs. Nixon's buggy. He lead her horse to the barn as she hurried across the porch and into the house. Amanda had already poured warm water into a bowl and had a towel ready for her hands, while Agnes quickly carried her basket upstairs. Grammaw and the little ones watched with big eyes and serious faces.

"Is Essie goin' to be all right, Miz Nixon?" Mike asked.

"I don't know," she answered. "We'll do all we can

and the Lord will decide. Mrs. Worthington, you pray, and the rest of you little ones find something to do outside, whatever will help most."

"Clean the yard," Agnes said. "Essie hates a messy yard."

The house was quiet after they left. Grammaw sat by the fire in her creaky rocker and twisted her gnarled hands together as she muttered a prayer. Amanda and Agnes cleared away the dishes and began to wash them without speaking. From upstairs they could hear Essie moan and an occasional word from Ma or Mrs. Nixon.

"What're they doin'?" Grammaw demanded to know. "What're they doin' all this long time? I never heard of a proper birthin' to take so long. Is somethin' wrong? Ag, you go up and ask, do!"

But Agnes shook her head, saying, "Nope, Grammaw. They'll tell us when there's somethin' to tell. Meantime, you keep prayin'. You're doin' just fine."

When the dishes were done Agnes started determinedly on the windows. They were streaked and dirty and certainly needed washing, but Amanda would have been inclined to let them go. It had been a long day and she had worked hard. Agnes wanted to keep on going, and indeed, it did seem to help. At every moan from above she scrubbed harder and the squeak of the vinegar soaked rag on the glass drowned out poor Essie's cries.

Agnes talked as she worked. It was as if she was dreaming aloud. She didn't seem to expect an answer.

"We'll make curtains, me and Essie. We'll get some nice goods and she'll cut it up right and we'll sew up the hems. We'll fix the place up pretty and people'll visit us and the baby'll have a cradle with a pretty quilt —"

Essie cried out then, in a voice so full of pain and despair that Amanda and Agnes were left trembling at the sound. Grammaw tried to get up from her chair.

"That's it!" she said excitedly. "Maybe the baby's borned!" They listened, but there was neither the whimper nor lusty cry of a new baby that Amanda had learned to expect. They could only wait.

After a long, long time Ma came slowly down the stairs.

"Essie's going to be all right," she said. "She's weak and tired and she'll need a lot of rest and good food, but she'll be all right. The baby — the little baby never lived. It was never able to breathe at all." Her eyes were full of tears. "We tried everything we knew, but it didn't do any good."

It was a sad trip homeward. The pale afternoon sun gave light but no warmth, and it set in a heavy sky that promised snow to come. Amanda rode with Mrs. Nixon, while Ma stayed on at the Worthingtons to keep a close eye on Essie for a few days.

"She needs good cooking," Ma had said, and Agnes answered eagerly, "I'll cook anything you say, ma'am, if you'll show me how. I want to take care of Essie."

The loss of the baby was hard on Agnes. She did not cry, although Amanda wept. Agnes's eyes were dry, but her thin shoulders sagged as if the burden was almost too much to bear. Ma put her arms around the girl and tried to comfort her, but Agnes was beyond comfort. After a while she said philosophically, "I guess it's all for the best. We probably couldn't have taken the right care of a little baby, messy and dirty as we are. But we're goin' to do better," she assured Ma. "We're goin' to get to be one of the nice families and some day Essie will marry a good fellow and have her baby right. And them little ones, they're goin' to amount to somethin' too."

"And what about you, Agnes?" Ma asked gently. Then the first tears trembled in Agnes's dark eyes.

"If I can make somethin' out of the rest of them, maybe I can do somethin' with myself. I don't say it will be easy, but I'm gonna try."

"You'll do it, Agnes," Amanda said. "You're the most determined person I ever knew. You'll grow up clean and pretty and smelling of lilac soap and people will know how nice you are."

"Be a long time afore people have anythin' good to say about a Worthington," Agnes said wryly.

" 'When a man's ways please the Lord, he maketh even his enemies to be at peace with him' ", Ma quoted. "You'll see."

"That's Bible," Agnes recognized it. "I'll keep a-sayin' that, and that other piece Amanda taught me, the Lord is my shepherd. I've got that one by heart. I'll never forget it."

Agnes stood on the porch and waved goodbye as Mrs. Nixon and Amanda drove away. "Will she be able to do it, do you think? Make something of the Worthingtons? It seems such a hopeless job."

"Nothing's hopeless, Amanda. She has spunk, that little Agnes, and pride, and love for her family even though she sees they need improvement. And she has you to stand by her now and be her friend. Nothing is hopeless when a man's ways please the Lord."

12

THE SNOW that the heavy clouds had promised was on the ground the next morning. Not deep yet, but piling up quickly. The flakes were fine and dry and settled thickly on the frozen earth.

"I wonder if I should let you go to school," Sarah worried at the bedroom window. "It looks as if we're in for a real storm."

"Oh, please do, Sarah," Mary begged. "If it gets bad Master Pulsifer will send us home early, and it's such fun when it snows. Besides," she added virtuously, "Ma doesn't like us to miss any more school than we have to." And Amanda put in, "I've already been out a day, and I don't want to fall behind."

"All right," Sarah gave in. "I'm planning to stay home with the young ones today and Hettie can take over tomorrow. I've got my books home. Just be sure to copy down the sums for me. Now dress warm, all of you. We'll have no nonsense with colds while Ma is gone."

With the efficiency born of long practice, they whipped into their clothes, out to do their chores, and in again to breakfast. It seemed odd without Ma, and Emily took advantage of the oddness to bubble in her mug of milk. This convulsed Teen and Toon, who were always ready to laugh anyway, and they made everyone else laugh. Teen seized the molasses pitcher and poured sticky golden spirals all over the pile of pancakes on her plate.

"I'm a spider! I'm spinning a web. See my web, Toon?"

Giggling, Toon reached for the pitcher to try it, but Sarah was too quick for her.

"Oh no you don't. There'll be no spiders at this table. Finish your breakfast with no more silliness and then wash your hands. You've molasses all over you."

They swallowed their giggles and their pancakes. Sarah was in charge when Ma was away and no one questioned her authority. They washed the breakfast dishes in a hurry and packed their dinner pails.

"Run along now and leave the beds. I'll do them after you've gone. It'll take you longer than usual to get to school, and you know Master Pulsifer doesn't like tardiness."

"He doesn't like wrong arithmetic, either," said Hettie gloomily, "and that's all I've got on my slate, one mistake after another."

"Stop your fussing," said Sarah firmly but goodhumoredly. "Now hurry." She tied scarves and wrapped mufflers and waved goodbye as they took their sled from the porch and started down the hill.

Up until that moment Amanda had been too busy to think very much about her experience of the day before.

There had been an unreal quality about it, and now, thinking back, it was hard to realize that so much had happened in one day. When she arrived home just at dusk the evening before she had been too tired and hungry to think. She ate her supper and tumbled immediately into bed, to fall into a restless sleep. This morning she felt tired and sad, and even the white sweep of trackless snow did not bring her pleasure. She thought of the cheerless uninviting kitchen that Agnes was probably trying to straighten, and of poor weary Essie and the thin neglected younger children.

And she thought, too, of what the girls at school would say. Alice Morris would stick her nose in the air, no doubt, and refuse to speak to anyone who befriended the unfortunate Worthingtons. And how would Dolly feel, and Ruthie, and even Julia?

Amanda walked on through the falling snow. Nan and Mary were frolicking in the drifts that were beginning to pile up along the lane. Hettie chose to sled down and had gone ahead in one glorious swoop, all the way to Three Corners. But Amanda plodded drearily along, burdened by her thoughts.

Julia and Thomas were waiting by their gate. Julia was prancing with impatience and cold. She had been waiting quite awhile, for the thick white flakes had settled on her hood and her curls like sugar sprinkled on a cooky.

"You've been forever getting here," she said. "I could hardly wait. You did go to the Worthingtons, Hettie said. Tell me about it. Was it awful? Are they terrible?"

All Amanda's misery seemed to well up inside her. She couldn't say a word, but she nodded as the tears started down her cheeks.

"Good gracious, Amanda! Was it that bad?"

"It was awful, Julia. They're so sad and neglected it's just pitiful. There's a girl named Agnes and we got to be friends, and she wanted to fix everything nice for the baby — and oh, Julia, the baby never even breathed! It was too little and weak."

Julia put a sympathetic arm around her.

"Don't cry, Amanda. It's over now and you don't ever have to think about them again if it makes you unhappy."

"Yes, I do, Julia. I have to think about them. I'm the only friend Agnes has — the only one she's ever had, I guess."

Julia stopped in the road and said, "Look me straight in the eye, Amanda Jane Scoville. Are you better friends with her or with me?" Amanda had to smile at that.

"With you, silly. You're my Best Friend, and you always will be." Julia smiled too.

"Then I'll be friends with this Agnes, too, and if she has two friends she won't be all alone in the world."

"Alice Morris said she couldn't like anyone who would even *speak* to a Worthington —"

"Pish-tush for Alice Morris. Who cares what she thinks? Come on, Amanda, the way you're dragging along, you might think it wasn't even snowing. If we hurry we can hit Alice with a snowball before the bell rings."

Julia might look as delicate as a sugar cooky but she

didn't act like one when the snow was falling. Amanda had to laugh. It was such a relief to know that Julia could even think of befriending poor Agnes. And what did it matter what Alice thought, anyway?

"I'll race you." Julia shook her head.

"Nothing doing. You always run faster than I do, and then I'll get there all out of breath and tired and I won't be able to hit the broad side of a barn. I have to preserve my aim, you know." She giggled as she trotted along with her curls bobbing on her shoulders. They looked around warily as they passed the Moore gate, but for once William and Henry weren't there to waylay them.

"My father says winter has really set in," Julia panted. "And it's about time. I can't be thankful at Thanksgiving if there's no snow on the ground."

Thanksgiving! Could it be almost here already? It was, of course, but the autumn had been such a busy one that Amanda didn't know where the days had gone. They'd better make some plans for Thanksgiving dinner. Ma might stay at the Worthingtons for some time yet.

A snowball that barely missed her shook all thoughts of Thanksgiving out of her mind. She and Julia stooped behind a big tree to make a few snowballs in advance. They would have to fight their way to the schoolhouse door, put their books and dinner pails inside and dash out again. They threw their small supply of snowballs as they zigzagged through the embattled schoolyard, but hampered as they were, their aim was not very accurate. They had hoped to go unnoticed until they were ready for action but Willam Moore spotted them and opened fire.

"We'll get him," Julia vowed as they put their books on the floor by the coat hooks. "He throws as wild as an old lady, that William. Come on, Amanda! Let's work our way over to the Touch Tree. We'll use it for protection until we can get a fort built at recess."

Every tree on the school ground had a name. There was the Climbing Tree, with low spreading branches, and the Playhouse Tree, with its gnarled roots — ideal for the youngest girls to use for the rooms of a house, with acorn cups and stone plates. The Touch Tree was a huge beech, the center of all the games like I Spy where a central safety spot was needed.

Ducking and running, Julia and Amanda dashed for the safety of its trunk, to lurk behind it until they had a few snowballs piled up ahead.

"We won't be able to storm their fort," Julia planned. "The bell's going to ring any minute now. All we can do is — ooh!"

Stubby Purcell had spotted the girls and while they were busy planning had slipped around the tree and pelted them both. The school bell started to ring then, and everyone, however reluctantly, filed into the school house.

Alice was already there with a group of girls who were timid about snowball fights. Nan and Mary were inside, too, for Sarah had insisted that Nan must change her damp clothes. Nan was drawing stick figures on her slate to amuse her seatmate, Annie McAllister. It was good to see shy little Nan taking the lead in some bit of fun. She was pink cheeked and laughing now, and her spindly little arms were beginning to fill out. We'll have plenty to be thankful about this Thanksgiving, Amanda thought. She was full of pleasant thoughts that evaporated as soon as she looked across the aisle at Alice Morris.

Alice was plainly ignoring her, with her sharp little nose stuck way up in the air to show her disdain. Everyone noticed. It was impossible not to, for Alice made it additionally plain by saying to Dolly,

"If you don't mind, I prefer to sit on the other side today."

Dolly moved over to the side of the double seat opposite Amanda and glanced nervously across the aisle. Dolly was a timid little thing who could be pushed one way or the other very easily. Alice liked her as a seatmate because Dolly did whatever she was told. Alice said, in a voice that was meant to carry, "Heaven knows what she may have brought back from the Worthingtons. I'd rather not sit too close."

Amanda flushed with embarrassment. Why did Alice have to be so mean? It wasn't fair. Julia heard too, of course. Everyone did, except perhaps Master Pulsifer. He was busy putting another piece of wood in the stove, from the pile that the big boys had stacked in the wood basket.

Alice was pleased with the attention her remark had caused and decided to continue. She wriggled in her seat and asked Dolly,

"Do you feel as if something's biting you? I wonder if those *things* can *jump* across the aisle?"

There were snickers here and there in the room. Few really liked Alice, yet they were quick enough to laugh at her unkind remarks. To Amanda's surprise, it was her old enemy Henry Moore who came to her defense.

"Some people I know better be careful if they go outside. The snow'll run down their stuck-up noses and drown'em."

William Moore was overcome by his brother's humor. He doubled up over his desk and shook with laughter. Others laughed too. Alice gave William an icy glance and remarked sweetly,

"Some people I know will be laughing out of the other sides of their faces when they find you-know-whats in their hair."

Several of the little girls squirmed uneasily in their seats and looked back over their shoulders at Amanda. The pebble of meanness that Alice had dropped was spreading ripples all over the room. Even Nan, who was normally a loving sweet-tempered child, shot a look of pure hatred at Alice. She nudged Annie and made a remark that Amanda knew must have been unkind. Amanda sat in the center of it all, her shoulders hunched miserably, as the class took sides for her or against her. She wondered if maybe Ma had been wrong to go to the Worthington house, if maybe it had all been a mistake. She was glad when Master Pulsifer stepped to his desk and opened the Bible. Surely when classes began everyone would be too busy for spitefulness.

It didn't happen that way, though. The big schoolroom usually hummed peaceably with the sound of murmured recitations. Today the hum was interrupted with whispers and quickly stifled bursts of laughter. When Amanda took her geography book to the front bench more than one girl moved out of her way as if there was danger of contamination.

Amanda's cheeks flamed. Ma had said that children could be cruel, but hadn't she also quoted, 'If a man's ways please the Lord, he maketh even his enemies be at peace with him.'?

Alice settled herself at the end of the bench so she would not have to sit next to Amanda. She made Dolly sit next to her to protect her. Sheep-like Dolly wasn't entirely happy as a buffer but Alice had her too well trained to protest.

Alice was needle-sharp in her recitation. She was a bright girl and always well prepared in class. She was much less likely to daydream and wool gather than Amanda, and her copybook and slate were neat and unspotted. Amanda was especially unprepared on this day. She had taken a school book along with her to the Worthingtons, but there had been so much else to think about that she had carried it back home again unopened. And in the evening she had been too sleepy to study. So when Master Pulsifer asked her to bound the state of New Hampshire, she stumbled along badly. Alice's hand was up immediately, and when the teacher nodded she rattled off the answer and then looked triumphantly at Amanda. Julia squeezed her hand under cover of the folds of her pinafore, but it was small comfort. At the next question, Ruthie Harrison hesitated. Before she could gather her wits together, Alice's hand shot up, and without waiting for the schoolmaster's nod, she gave the answer. Ruthie had shown where her loyalty lay by sitting close to Amanda on the other side. She glared at Alice and burst out,

"You didn't have to be in such a hurry! I knew the answer — I just couldn't think of it!"

Master Pulsifer looked at the little group on the recitation bench before him. They sat there stiff as pokers, anger sticking out all over them. First there was Alice and next to her Dolly. Henry was between Dolly and Julia and next to Julia was Amanda and then Ruthie and Albert and Steuben.

Albert was for Amanda, or rather, against Alice. He had disliked Alice ever since he had put a small mouse in her dinner pail. The resulting uproar had been beautiful to hear, but Alice had reported him to the teacher. He was still working out his punishment three weeks later and he resented it.

Stubby Purcell was neutral for the time being. He couldn't stand Alice, but he wasn't overfond of Amanda, either. She had washed his face with snow on the day of the first snowfall and he found it hard to forgive her, although his plan had been to do the same to her. Stubby was waiting to see which way things would go before he took sides.

Master Pulsifer sighed and asked another question. No one was concentrating. When he said, "Tell me in detail how you would travel from Boston, Massachusetts to Atlanta, Georgia. What states would you pass through, what rivers and mountains would you cross?" they all stared blankly ahead.

"Dolly?" he asked. "Steuben? Albert? Alice?" Alice tried but she had missed the first part of the question.

"Henry was whispering," she alibied. "I couldn't hear."

Henry was enraged. Perhaps he foresaw three weeks of punishment for him, too. At any rate he turned red as a beet and gave poor Dolly a giant shove. She was pushed against Alice, hard, and Alice flew off the end of the bench with a thump, with Dolly on top of her. The long bench was suddenly lightened at one end. Stubby and Albert went down and the bench rose as everyone started to slide.

Master Pulsifer moved quickly to balance the bench, but Stubby was already off on the floor. Ruthie's high-pitched voice rose in a startled squeal. Alice and Dolly writhed on the floor in an effort to get untangled and seated again. Laughter exploded all over the room, but was instantly hushed as the students waited to see what Master Pulsifer would do about such a commotion. He was looking his angriest, and waited in stern silence until the geography class was once more sitting motionless in front of him.

"You may return to your seats." His voice was icy cold. Master Pulsifer was a kind teacher but he believed in firm discipline. The eight scholars returned fearfully to their places and waited for him to speak. There was a long uncomfortable pause while he gathered his thoughts.

"This has been a disgraceful occurrence. I trust that nothing like this will ever again happen in my classroom. Unhappily, I fear that the spirit of unkindness which prompted this behavior is widespread throughout the school. In place of individual punishment, which you all understand is well deserved, I have decided on a different approach. All classes will be suspended for the rest of the morning. There will be no recess. Each of you, even the youngest, will write a composition, the subject of which will be the meaning of the Golden Rule. You do know the Golden Rule, I believe? Yes? There was little evidence of it in school this morning. Well then, get to work. I expect this to be the best composition you have ever written. You will, of course, pay attention to grammar and spelling and neatness. But above all, I want you to think. Think of how 'Do Unto Others' applies to you and to your classmates. You will work in silence, without consulting your seatmates. You may begin."

For almost two hours the schoolroom was quiet. There was only the sound of squeaking slate pencils and the occasional shuffles of feet as Master Pulsifer's students struggled to marshall their ideas.

"Do unto others as you would have others do unto you." Amanda wrinkled her forehead and tried to think what to write. At first her sentences were jumbled and stilted, but as she worked along her ideas began to flow. She would write about the Worthingtons, she decided. She poured all her feelings into it. She wrote that Ma had been following the Golden Rule when she went to help Essie Worthington, just as others had when they had come to help the Scovilles. As she wrote, her mind cleared of its uncertainty. She knew, just as surely as Ma had known, that what they had done was right, and that somehow others would come to see that it was right. "When a man's ways please the Lord," she quoted, and she knew that it was true. Best of all, Amanda decided, The Lord makes a man be at peace with himself. She felt quiet and calm and happy, although her slate pencil finger had a blister on it.

When her slate was full she copied the words neatly in her copybook, then cleaned her slate and wrote some more. By the time she finally finished, it was noon. Her stomach was growling with hunger and her fingers were cramped from clutching slate pencil and pen. The younger children had long ago turned in their copybooks to Master Pulsifer. One by one the pupils rose and tiptoed up to lay their compositions on the teacher's desk and then tiptoed back to their seats and studied in silence. When the last copybook was on the pile in front of him, he rose and announced,

"You may open your dinner pails now. I will finish reading your compositions during noon hour."

It was a quiet dinner hour. There was very little talking. Every eye was on Master Pulsifer as he opened and read one book after another. There was nothing in his expression to tell if he was pleased or not with what he read. After all, writing a composition was a much lighter punishment than a birching all around. The long birch rod stood in the corner, reminding them that the teacher could change his mind if he wanted to.

The snow had been falling steadily all morning and was still coming down. The windows were steamed over with the heat from the iron stove. The stove was the loudest noise-maker in the hushed schoolroom. It crackled and sizzled and kept up a merry conversation with itself.

At last, after what seemed like forever, Master Pulsifer cleared his throat.

"I have found not a few mistakes in spelling," he said. "I have made a list of the misspelled words and we will include them in a spelling test soon. I find your grasp of grammatical principles uncertain. Some hard work is indicated in this area. But on the whole the ideas expressed are good ones. I am proud of you. These are not easy ideas to live up to, I will grant you. But I trust that you will try. And now, let us wrap up warm and go outside for the rest of the noon recess. I think perhaps a snowball fight is in order to air out our dusty brains."

They all gasped. Here they had been nervously waiting for a severe punishment, maybe even a birching, and what did Master Pulsifer suggest? A snowball fight!

They hurried into their coats before the schoolmaster could change his mind. If he wanted a snowball fight, they would give him one. There was no time for fort building. It was every man for himself, with trees and the corner of the schoolhouse serving as cover.

Julia took command of the girls' side and Johnny Jamison led the boys. Everyone joined in, even the girls who usually stayed close to the schoolhouse door and the young ones who customarily preferred sledding to snowballing. It was a fair fight, too, no sneaking meanness,

just everyone making fat snowballs and throwing them. Alice clipped Henry with a good one, and Julia laughed.

"Good for you, Alice! We'll teach those boys a lesson. Come on, don't hang back now, we've got them on the run."

For once Alice wasn't prim or prissy, but working hard with the rest. It might not last, but it was a good sign.

Stubby caught Amanda and washed her face with snow, and that was all right, too. Another day she would get even with him, maybe get mad about it, but today was different. Today it was part of the game. At last Master Pulsifer looked at his watch and announced that recess was over. It was hard to tell which side had won. Neither, really, or both. Maybe everyone had come out ahead. Amanda tried to sort it out in her mind as she stamped the snow off her shoes and dried her skirt before the fire.

Something had happened to the unpleasantness of the morning, but where had it gone? Into the copybooks still piled on the teacher's desk, or into the snowballs, or gently washed away by the falling snow? She couldn't decide.

13

MA CAME HOME the day before Thanksgiving.

"I wanted to get away sooner, but I knew you were doing fine here. Mrs. Nixon drove over a couple of times in their sleigh to bring me the news — and they really needed help."

"Tell," Mary begged. "Tell us all about it, every word."

They sat by the fire after supper, eating crisp cold apple slices as fast as Ma could cut them up. There was no school the next day and no homework. Sarah had gone ahead with the Thanksgiving preparations without Ma. She had baked four lovely pies, two pumpkin and two apple. They were in the pantry cupboard now, along with a bowl of applesauce and jars of fancy picklestuff that Hettie had brought up from the cellar storehouse. There was a fat chicken hanging outside in the cold, high enough so no fox could jump and reach it. Tomorrow Ma would roast it slowly in the oven with sweet potatoes and light puffy biscuits. Amanda swallowed and reached for another apple slice as she thought of the Thanksgiving dinner.

"Yes, Ma, tell us all about the Worthingtons. Start at the beginning."

"You all know the beginning — how I had to wrestle with my conscience and make up my mind to go. Well, I've one more thing to be thankful about tomorrow. I'm thankful I went when Eph Worthington came. Oh girls, you never saw a more neglected family! The mother died four years ago when the youngest one was only a baby. I guess they've all run wild ever since. The grandmother tries to keep some order, but she's old and cranky and bent over with rheumatism. They're ignorant and shiftless and dirty — all the things people have said about them — but there's a spark of goodness in them and that little Agnes is working hard to fan the spark into a roaring fire. She's made up her mind that the Worthington family will amount to something. I think she's going to make it happen. When Preacher Ewing came for the burial — yes, he came — Mrs. Nixon had a good talk with him and I guess she made him unthink a few thoughts — when he came, they were almost awed. They thought they were beyond hope and had given up. He preached a good sermon for the baby, best one I've ever heard him preach, all gentle and soft. Agnes had bullied and pushed and driven the others into cleaning up. We washed and ironed and mended what clothes they have. It won't happen overnight, you know nothing big ever does, but the day will come when the Worthingtons will be accepted as good neighbors."

Amanda asked, "How is Essie?"

"Essie is still weak and frail and can't help much, but I believe she's struggling to rebuild her wayward life. She'll come along fine. Eph and his father finally got the cupboard door fixed and now they're working on those broken chairs. I taught Agnes what I could about cooking and got her started on Thanksgiving dinner. I knew you'd be all right here so I stayed long enough to clean a couple of chickens and do some baking. But you'll never know how glad I am to be home again, here in our nice clean house with all my nice clean girls!"

Emily stirred sleepily on Ma's lap and stuffed another apple slice in her mouth. "Don't go away again, Ma," she said. "We like to have you home."

"I hope I won't have to go away soon. But if I'm called you know I have to go."

Emily begged for her froggie song so they sang all the verses. They were out of breath and laughing when they finished.

"Oh Ma, it is good to have you home again. Now we can be really thankful tomorrow." Amanda sighed and leaned against Ma's knee. "I feel so happy I could bust wide open."

Ma laughed. "Let's all get to bed before you do bust wide open. I've had a long day and so have you, and we have a busy day ahead of us tomorrow."

Hettie grumbled a little about going to bed with the chickens, but even she was sleepy. Amanda undressed in a happy glow. It was so nice to have all the family together again, and the world so right. At this thought she felt a sudden icy chill. The family wasn't all together. They never would be, not with Pa gone. How could she forget? And how could she forget the misery of the Worthington family and feel that the world was right?

Hettie and Sarah and Mary were almost asleep. Mary grunted drowsily as Amanda slipped out of bed and started down the stairs to the kitchen. Ma was still up. Amanda could hear her pushing the still smoldering logs to the back of the fireplace where sparks could not fly out during the night. Ma turned, startled, as Amanda came into the room.

"Why, baby, what are you doing up so late, and in your bare feet! You'll freeze. Now, what's wrong? Why that long face?"

"Ma, I feel so awful!" The quick tears welled in her eyes. "I was thinking of how happy I am — and I forgot all about Pa, and Essie's baby, and all the sad things —"

Ma scooped her up, big girl that she was, and sat down in her rocking chair. She cuddled Amanda on her lap as if she were as young as Emily.

"No reason you shouldn't be joyful, child. You are glad for what we have, not for what we've lost."

"But —"

"Happiness is more than just laughing and joking, Amanda. I think maybe happiness is going through the dark forest of sorrow and out to the sunlight on the other side. And knowing, even in the darkest time, that there surely will be sunlight there."

They rocked quietly for a long time while Amanda thought this over. The Scovilles had gone through a long dark forest when it had seemed as if they would never see the sunlight again. But they were coming out again into the light, weren't they? So it was only right to be a little glad.

Amanda had almost dozed off in her mother's lap when she heard Ma whisper, "Up to bed now, baby. Morning comes early." She yawned as she kissed Ma goodnight for the second time that evening and went groggily up to bed. She put her cold feet on Mary's fat little warm ones and in a moment was fast asleep.

It was snowing again when they awoke next morning. "Happy Thanksgiving," Ma called from downstairs. "Happy Thanksgiving and Happy Snowfall." The new snow coming on top of the recent heavy fall made the drifts too deep for church going. So after the chores and breakfast were over Ma had a Bible reading time. They sang their favorite hymns and talked awhile about the many things for which they were thankful.

"I like this kind of day," Hettie said. "Quiet and peaceful and happy. If this snow keeps up we could be snowbound until Christmas."

"Christmas!" Sarah was surprised. "Does anyone realize that Christmas is almost here? It'll be on us before we know it, the way time goes by so fast. I haven't even given it a thought."

Sarah wasn't the only one who was surprised. There had been so much to do every day that none of them had planned ahead to Christmas. It had seemed so far off and now it was almost here. Amanda resolved that in her first free moment she would make a list. The free moment did not come until after their Thanksgiving dinner was over, and the dishes were cleared away and washed.

"Let's do our evening chores early," Ma suggested. "It will be dark early with all this snow falling. The animals will be glad to settle down sooner than usual. If we shovel a path to the barn it will be partly snowed over by morning, but even so, it will ease the shoveling tomorrow."

"I can shovel," said Teen.

"Me too," said Toon and Emily.

"Tell you what," Hettie said, "let's all help. It will be good to get out and run off some of that good dinner. I feel like a stuffed chicken myself."

So they all wrapped up warm and went out to shovel and run and flounder in the drifts until all nine of them looked like snowmen. And when the path was shovelled and the pigs and chickens and Royal George were fed and the cow milked, when Betsy and Biteser had been given their evening saucer of milk, then the nine snowmen came into the house for the night.

"We'll have a bite to eat later on, but let's not bother with a real supper." Ma put another log on the fire and settled down in her rocker to knit. She worked awhile and then began to think out loud.

"Mittens for Agnes and the little Worthingtons — will I ever have time?"

"I'll help on the hand part of the mittens, Ma, if you'll do the thumbs. I just hate turning thumbs and heels."

"That'll be a big help, Hettie, since time is so short. You must learn to do thumbs sometime, though. It's part of a woman's education."

Hettie snorted. "Like arithmetic. Well, I'll labor through thumbs and sums, I suppose, but I'll never learn to like either of them."

Amanda sat at one end of the table, far enough away from the others that they couldn't see what she was writing. She wrinkled her forehead as she thought. What would she make for Christmas for Ma? After struggling with that for awhile she went on to Mary. Mary should be easy, but wasn't. And Nan — ? She had no success at all until she wrote down Teen and Toon and Emily. Their gifts would be clothes for the dolls she had made them last summer. Amanda had promised them outfits months ago but she had never found time to make them. She thought again about Ma and the rest and then gave up. Ideas would come to her, she was sure, but there wasn't much time.

Nan must have been puzzling about Christmas gifts, too, for she slid along the bench and whispered, "Manda, you've got to help me. I don't know what to do about presents."

Amanda admitted that she was stumped, except for the youngest ones. "I aim to make three sets of doll clothes, little pants and petticoats, too. Ma'll have some fine white cloth."

Nan was suddenly struck with a thought. She urged Amanda to let her share the doll clothes present.

"I can take small neat stitches, Manda, you know I can. And what if I make some tatted lace, little bitsy fine lace for the underthings? Wouldn't that be good?"

Amanda agreed that it would be, but that still left a long list of presents to think about. Mary was already at work on a secret project that she covered with her apron every time anyone came near. It was a sewing project, for she had her little workbasket out by her side. Hettie was busy with a list, too. She kept writing and crossing out and blotting the back page of her copybook, but evidently she made up her mind at last, for by bedtime she was smiling, looking like Biteser when he had stalked a mouse and caught it.

In the days before Thanksgiving they had not thought about Christmas at all. In the days that came after, they thought of nothing else in their rush to get ready. A certain amount of time had to be set aside for chores, inside and out, and for school work. But when these things were done, every spare minute was spent in all sorts of secret activities. It was difficult to keep anything secret in so small a house. It was often necessary for Amanda to turn her eyes away when she was dying to look, or to pretend that she didn't know what was going on when Ma flipped her apron over the work in her lap. With so many Scovilles milling around in the house it would have been easy to ferret out anything if she had wanted to try. But the surprise was the best part of the whole thing.

"If only Christmas came in the summer time," Mary complained. "We could go off to the woods or the barn and hide. But where can we hide in here? Upstairs is too cold unless you're in bed and that leaves this room and the downstairs bedrooms."

They managed somehow. Nan and Amanda did their schoolwork early so that they could close their books the minute Teen and Toon and Emily went to bed. The doll clothes went slowly, even with two pairs of hands working on them. Amanda cut little underpants and petticoats out of the soft white cloth Ma had given her, and Nan's fingers flew at her tatting until she had several yards of lace to sew on the hems of the petticoats.

"Aren't they dear?" Sarah smiled from her loom as Nan held them up. "But will you ever get three outfits done in time? We could use one of Mr. Aaron's sewing machines now."

"We'd run it until it was red hot," Amanda said. "Doll clothes take almost as long to make as people clothes. I hope I have time to put pockets on the pinafores. I don't want to do it on one if I can't do it on all of them. The little me-toos want everything to be alike."

"Why don't we all work on the doll clothes?" Hettie asked. "We could each contribute something and make a really splendid present."

Mary eagerly offered to make tiny handkerchiefs for the pinafore pockets, with tiny flowers embroidered on them. Mary's embroidery was not too neat yet, but she loved to do it. Ma said she would find some velvet scraps and make little hoods and shawls. Hettie said, "I despise taking tiny stitches, but just this once, I'll try. Toss over a pair of pants and I'll work on them."

The days spun by. Amanda could feel the lovely excited feeling building up inside her, as if the waiting and the secrets were almost too much for her. Ma was busy with preparations too. Often they came home from school to find the house scented with cinnamon and cloves and nutmeg. The little ones would be bursting to tell, and would go around with their hands over their mouths to make sure they didn't forget and spillover all the wonderful things they knew.

With everything else, the house had to be cleaned and made ready. Ma scrubbed the floor with sand to scour and whiten the wide floor boards. They cut spruce boughs from the woodlot and fastened them over the door to perfume the room with their fresh clean smell of outdoors. Ma said they should have a tree — not a big one, for they did not have much to hang on it — so Hettie and Sarah made a trip to the woodlot to find a small well-shaped evergreen of just the right size. They selected a dear little tree, round and fat and no taller than the twins, and set it up in the corner. It was far enough from the fire to be safe from any stray sparks, but near enough that the firelight flickered on its green boughs.

"We'll make strings of popcorn to drape all over it. Yes, you may help string," she said to Teen and Toon, and "yes, Emily, you may help hang the strings on the tree."

Last Christmas had been such a strained, sad, worried one that it hardly seemed like a holiday at all. Pa was gone, and the blizzards had drifted them in so deep that it was all they could do to get to the barn and feed the animals. There was no question of going further up the mountain to the woods for a tree. Hettie and Sarah and Ma chopped wood, not for decorations, but for the fuel to keep them from freezing. Nan still had been so weak and frail that no one was quite sure she would manage to get through the bitter winter. It was so different last year, Amanda thought. If only Pa were here this would be the happiest Christmas we've ever had. And if Mr. Aaron could come, and Mr. O'Leary with his fiddle — what a time they would have then! She sighed. It couldn't be, of course, but wouldn't it be wonderful?

Mrs. Nixon stopped in one day to visit. Little as she was, she had managed to struggle up the steep snowy lane to say that she was planning a visit to the Worthingtons the first day her sons could spare the sleigh. Ma had five pairs of warm mittens to send along, some jars of fruit and pickles and a basket of cookies.

"It's not much," she apologized, "but we didn't have a lot of time."

"Took some fast knitting to get this many done," Mrs. Nixon said. "I got Clara and Ethel knitting too. Between us, we made a shawl for Grammaw Worthington, a good warm gray one, and a right pretty one for Essie. That Clara, her knitting's no better'n her cooking, but she was willing. I'll say that for her. Anyway, it'll be more Christmas than the Worthingtons have had for a long time."

Amanda wished there was something special she could send to Agnes. New mittens were fine, and she knew they'd be welcome, but wasn't there something they could add that would be more than just useful? It was Ma who thought of it. "Let's send Agnes our other cake of lilac soap. She admired it so, and she has so little."

They all agreed, but it was with a slight twinge that Amanda saw the gay wrapper packed away in the basket. She had to remind herself firmly that it is more blessed to give than to receive.

The Christmas excitement was spread to the school, too. Alice spoke loftily of the presents she expected to receive, much grander than any the Scovilles were giving or getting. But it didn't matter a bit. Amanda and Julia smiled at one another. At Christmas time even Alice Morris didn't bother them.

At home Ma said Amanda was so excited she was impossible, but she said it with a smile so it couldn't have been too bad. After a lot of puzzling, Amanda had decided on a food gift for Mary, since her plump little sister was so fond of eating. She planned to make a batch of brown sugar candy with butternuts on top, one of Mary's favorites. Shelling the butternuts was no problem. She took them out to the barn where she could crack and pick them out in private. But how on earth would she manage to make a batch of penuche without Mary catching on? Ma solved that.

"Let's make penuche this evening," she suggested. "Mrs. Nixon has a sweet tooth for an old lady."

So they killed two birds with one stone, and Mary never suspected that half of the candy was intended for her. She eyed it appreciatively when it was poured out on the big platter and cut into squares, and remarked that they'd never made better. But she didn't suspect.

That left Sarah and Hettie and Nan and Ma and precious little time. It was when she saw Hettie and Sarah both reaching out to use the same pincushion that she knew what she would do. Pincushions all around. Ma had scraps of velvet and silk and ribbon — nothing like that was ever thrown away — and even a little piece of black ball fringe left from Ma's pelisse. Little round fancy pincushions, every one different, and they could be hung on the tree.

The day before Christmas Mr. Hopkinson's sleigh came jingling up the lane. He had a strong young team and they came up the steep road almost as easily as if it had been level. He was delivering Ma's carpet. The Hopkinson children, Annie and Ella and Catherine and Alben came along for the ride. The little girls shrieked with joy at the sight of Hettie and Amanda, and immediately wanted to play tag. Mary and Nan and the three smallest Scovilles put on their coats and ran out to play. Hettie and Amanda and Sarah stayed in to help with the carpet.

"Aim to lay it, too," said jolly Mr. Hopkinson. "Got orders from my wife not to come home without tackin' down your carpet strips."

Ma said she was sure they could manage, but Mr. Hopkinson wouldn't hear of it. He pushed back furniture and undid the heavy rolls and began pounding in carpet tacks almost before they knew what he was about. Alben helped, but Amanda noticed that he was careful always to keep his father between him and the door, as if he was uneasy about something.

The carpet was beautiful, just beautiful. The many different colored strips of cloth all blended into the prettiest carpet they had ever seen. They could pick out pieces of faded red that had been cast-off flannel petticoats, and a dull blue that was Ma's old wool wrapper, discarded when it finally fell all to pieces. The carpet was thick and soft and bright and it covered the bare boards of the floor from corner to corner, with only a space left clear by the hearth, for fear of flying sparks.

Ma's eyes shone with pleasure. The carpet was not only lovely to look at, it would keep out the drafts that came up through the cracks in the floor. When the bitterest days of winter came, they would be prepared.

Sarah had finished the flower painting for Mrs. Hopkinson's frame and when the red-faced, panting children came in to admire the carpet, they admired Sarah's flowers too. Ma passed around cookies but young Alben wasn't hungry, it seemed. He kept a close eye on Mary as if she might suddenly turn and pull all his hair out. Hettie looked at Amanda with an impish grin. They both knew what was on Alben's mind.

After the Hopkinsons had left, Ma sat down in her rocker, all out of breath with excitement.

"This is my Christmas present right here. It's everyone's present. We all contributed with our cutting and rolling strips, and what a wonderful gift it is."

Ma put a burlap bag down by the door for a doormat

and another one out on the porch. "Now do be careful and scrape your feet well before you step on the carpet. We want it to be pretty and clean for visitors." Ma couldn't have guessed in a million years who their first visitor would be.

The visitor came after supper that evening. The younger ones were sitting on the hearth stringing popcorn just as fast as Hettie could pop it, being careful not to let a single grain spill on the new carpet. Sarah was clacking away on her little table loom, Nan and Mary and Amanda were singing. What with the noise of the loom, the crackling fire, the popping corn and the singing, the first knock on the door went unnoticed. It came again, louder this time. A voice called,

"Von't you let a poor traveler in?"

All the bustle stopped suddenly. Amanda breathed, "It can't be! It surely can't be —" and then she raced to open the door. It was. It was Mr. Aaron standing there on the porch. She stared as if she was seeing a ghost, but if it was a ghost he was a plump, well fed apparition, so bundled up in his greatcoat and warm cap that only his nose was out in the cold.

"Vell, Amanda Jane, do I come in?" he asked. His deep jolly voice rumbled out of the wrappings of mufflers. She was too surprised to answer, just held the door open while he stamped the snow from his boots. Once he was inside she found her voice.

"Mr. Aaron! Mr. Aaron!" she shrieked. "You've come for Christmas!"

The others were shrieking too. Even Ma was hugging

Mr. Aaron and wiping away her happy tears at the same time. It was an uproarious greeting and left no doubt about his welcome. When they were all convinced that it *was* Mr. Aaron, that he was real and standing there, that he had somehow managed to arrive for Christmas, they remembered their manners. They helped him off with his knapsack and his coat, and led him to the place of honor in front of the fire. Ma made him a cup of tea and cut a piece of molasses cake and shook her head at the eager children who clustered around him.

"No questions until Mr. Aaron has a chance to warm up and rest," she said, "though I'll admit I'm as curious as you are."

They waited impatiently until he had finished his cake and tea, and then Mary said, "Now tell, please."

He told them the whole story, how he had decided just the week before that he wanted to spend Christmas with the Scovilles, and he made up his mind that snow and wintery weather would not stand in his way. His niece had protested, but he packed a few things in his knapsack and came anyway.

"Did you bring your wagon?"

He shook his head. "Dobbin and the vagon vould never be able to get through the snow. No, I took the cars from Philadelphia to Vilkes Barre, and vas lucky enough to be offered sleigh rides most of the rest of the vay."

Then there was excitement all over again. None of them had even seen a railroad, much less ridden on one, and to think that Mr. Aaron had come all that way on a train!

"A bumpy, noisy, dirty vay to travel, if you vant to know my opinion. I much prefer my horse and vagon for comfort. But it vas speedy — ve flew like the vind vherever the tracks vere clear."

It was *so* nice to have him there. He sat in the high backed chair that had been Pa's and filled part of that aching emptiness. All of a sudden it seemed more like Christmas now that he was there with them. He wanted to know all that had happened since he saw them last and they told him about everything. He had had a letter from Mr. O'Leary. All was well with their young friend. He was painting — more signs than portraits, it was true, but still enough portraits to encourage him. He was in Baltimore and would stay there as long as the commissions kept coming. He was working hard and living quietly in a small boarding house — he had exchanged a portrait for his meals — and was managing to save a little money.

It was like a Christmas gift to get the news about Mr. O'Leary. It was the next best thing to seeing him. Amanda's holiday heart was full to overflowing.

The little tree stood in the corner, trimmed with the strings of popcorn. Mr. Aaron's eyes twinkled as he looked at it.

"A very nice tree," he said, "but a trifle bare, don't you think?"

Their faces fell slightly. They thought it looked so pretty. "I guess it's not what you're used to seeing in the city," Amanda said. "I guess they have things fancy in Philadelphia."

"I haf seen them so." He nodded. "Vith stars and gilt and angels. Very fancy. Vill you bring me my knapsack, Hettie? I haf a small gift for your Christmas tree."

Hettie took his knapsack down from the back of the door. He unstrapped it carefully and reached inside.

"I packed lightly for such a long trip. I knew that some of the vay I vould haf to go on foot, and I am too old a man to carry a heavy load. So I brought only vun gift — something to be shared by all. Let us hope that the jiggling railroad has not broken — no, all is vell. Here it is, and a very merry Christmas, my dears."

He handed a box to Ma and she lifted the lid wonderingly. There, nestled in tissue paper were wax angels and birds and glass balls so delicate and shimmering it seemed they might break at the merest breath. Blue and red and green — they had never seen anything so lovely. There was a hunting horn and silvery glass icicles, and for the top of the tree a golden star.

Ma hung them on the tree and stood back. The ornaments sparkled and shone in the firelight, and the loops of popcorn looked like new-fallen snow. There wasn't anything to say. They just looked and looked at their lovely little tree.

There were richer homes, maybe, and somewhere there were taller trees, but you couldn't have convinced the Scovilles of that. Amanda thought of the pincushions ready to be hung on the tree, and Mary's penuche put away in the cupboard, and the three dolls she would dress as soon as Teen and Toon and Emily were in bed, and all the other secrets the house was hiding. Her holiday heart was beating fast as she said, speaking for all of them,

"Let Christmas come. The Scovilles are ready."